T5-DID-123

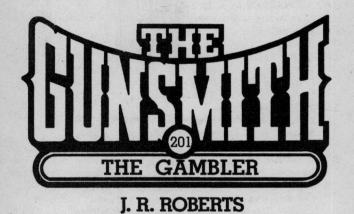

THE GUNSMITH

201

THE GAMBLER

J. R. ROBERTS

JOVE BOOKS, NEW YORK

THE GAMBLER

A Jove Book / published by arrangement with
the author

PRINTING HISTORY
Jove edition / October 1998

The Penguin Putnam Inc. World Wide Web site address is
http://www.penguinputnam.com

ISBN: 0-515-12373-0

A JOVE BOOK®
Jove Books are published by The Berkley Publishing Group,
a member of Penguin Putnam Inc.,
375 Hudson Street, New York, New York 10014.
JOVE and the "J" design are trademarks
belonging to Jove Publications, Inc.

PRINTED IN THE UNITED STATES OF AMERICA

10 9 8 7 6 5 4 3 2 1

PROLOGUE

Water Hole started out as just that, a water hole. It was Jedediah Weaver who got the idea to build a town around it. The miners in the area needed someplace to come to drink, eat, gamble, and buy supplies. Weaver was thirty-five, had been a gambler all his life. What could be a bigger gamble, he thought, than to try to build a whole town?

The gold strike in California Gulch, Colorado, was huge, and Weaver decided to bet on it. He'd stop traveling from game to game and build a town, where the games would come to him.

It started with the saloon, which he called the Crystal Palace. In the beginning there was no crystal anywhere, and it certainly didn't look like a palace. In fact, it started out as a tent, most of Weaver's initial investment going into tables, chairs, lamps, and a real mahogany bar. A tent was good enough in the beginning to keep the elements away while the miners and gamblers passed their money to him across a poker table.

Later he hired a faro dealer and installed a roulette wheel. By the end of the first year he had taken in enough gold to actually build a real saloon out of wood. No crystal yet, and it still wasn't a palace, but it was getting closer.

• • •

A saloon was only the first step. Other buildings began popping up around the Crystal Palace and throughout the Gulch, some of them nothing but shacks, others built partly of wood and partly of burlap. They offered a variety of services: gunsmithing, tanning, carpentry—which would be in more and more demand as time went on. But Weaver knew he needed to give the miners another reason to come to his "town." In order for it to be a real town, attracting more men, it needed to have three things. One was a saloon, and he had that. The second was a general store—complete with a post office—so the miners would have someplace to buy supplies and mail letters to their wives and sweethearts back home. And third, it needed women. Oh, not the proper kind, but soiled doves or, to be more blunt, whores.

Jed Weaver decided to work on the general store next. He knew nothing of running such a venture, so with infinite wisdom heretofore infrequently displayed, he needed to take on a partner.

Here the vaunted Weaver luck, still going strong, came into play when he took a marker in a poker game from a man named Harvey Larch. Larch was a storekeeper by trade who had given up his business to go hunting for gold. He was, however, by his own admission, a piss-poor miner, and up until the time he got into a poker game with Jedediah Weaver, was thinking of going back home.

Four tens got in his way, though. They appeared in his hand magically when he drew three cards to a pair of tens, and so enamored of them was he that he signed a marker when he could not match Jed Weaver's bet dollar for dollar. When Weaver accepted the marker and laid down his straight flush, Larch knew he was in trouble. He dropped his cards facedown on the table.

• • •

"I can't honor that marker, Mr. Weaver," Larch said later, in Weaver's office in the back of the saloon. Weaver sat behind his huge cherry wood desk, specially ordered from Philadelphia, regarding Mr. Harvey Larch critically.

"Then why did you sign a marker, Mr. Larch?"

"Because I had four tens."

Weaver looked over at his friend and right-hand man Oliver Quinn. Quinn, a large man with wide shoulders and narrow hips, also served as chief enforcer for the Crystal Palace. When anyone became rowdy and interfered with the smooth fleecing of gold from the miners, Quinn would step in and take care of the situation.

Quinn raised his eyebrows at Weaver and shrugged. Weaver thought his friend's broad shoulders might burst the seams of his black, broadcloth jacket. Weaver himself never had to worry about such things, being a man who was more bones than skin.

"That's a damned good reason, Mr. Larch," Weaver said, giving rise to a hopeful look on the man's face, but quickly dashing it by saying, "but the fact is, you signed a marker you cannot honor. There are several ways we can handle this matter."

"W-what are they?" Larch, a man of insignificant stature, had watery eyes, and Weaver could not recall if they had been that way the whole time, or if the man was on the verge of tears.

"Well, I could turn you over to Mr. Quinn, here, who would make sure that you are never again able to sign a bad marker."

Larch looked at Quinn and shuddered, imagining the horrible damage such a man might inflict on his body.

"W-what other options do we have?"

"You could work it off," Weaver said.

Larch's watery eyes brightened.

"How can I do that?"

"I don't know. Can you deal faro?"

"No."

"Spin a roulette wheel?"

"No."

"Tend bar?"

"N-no."

"Cook?"

"No."

Weaver leaned forward.

"Mr. Larch, you are making it very difficult for me to be decent about this matter."

"C-couldn't you turn me over to the law?"

"The law is something we don't yet have here in Water Hole."

"T-then, w-what do we do?"

"You tell me, Mr. Larch," Weaver said, "you tell me."

Larch opened his mouth, but no words were forthcoming.

Finally, he cleared his throat and croaked, "I . . . don't . . . know."

"Well, tell me, Mr. Larch," Weaver said, "before coming west to try your hand at mining, what did you do? What was your profession?"

"I—I'm a shopkeeper," Larch stammered. "I had my own mercantile."

"Mercantile," Weaver said thoughtfully, "is that like a general store?"

"Yes, sir."

Weaver looked over at Quinn, who smiled.

"Mr. Larch," Weaver said, "we might be able to do business, after all."

So Jed Weaver had his general store. His partner—albeit owner of only five percent of the business—Harvey Larch would operate the store, and Weaver found yet another way to funnel the miners' gold dust into his pockets.

He already had a freight line that delivered his beer and whiskey and—of course—cards and chips to his saloon, so it was very easy to start using them to stock the store with supplies.

Now Weaver could move onto his third objective—getting Water Hole its whorehouse.

There were already cribs set up here and there, but the poor pathetic creatures who plied their trade there were more likely to give a man crabs—or worse—than any kind of satisfaction. Weaver wanted to set up a clean, well-run establishment which he, of course, would own. The money the miners didn't lose in his saloon, or spend in his store, would be left here with the soiled doves.

But first he needed to find someone who would run the place, then he needed to build it, and finally to stock it with clean, professional women.

For the first part he decided to travel to Denver—and that's where he ran into his old friend, Clint Adams.

ONE

Denver, Colorado, was only a few days ride south of California Gulch. A hard ride by buggy or buckboard, but a fairly easy trip on a good horse. Denver, as a city, was a gambler's dream, and Weaver had been there many times. He stayed where he usually did, at the Denver House Hotel, and he meant to take as much time as he needed to find what he wanted. After all, it wasn't as if he had left behind a claim that could be jumped in his absence, and he trusted his friend, Oliver Quinn, to run the saloon while he was gone.

He was crossing the lobby of the Denver House when he saw a familiar figure standing at the front desk.

"Checking in, or out?" a voice asked behind Clint.

While the voice was familiar, he couldn't quite place it until he turned around.

"Jed Weaver?"

Weaver smiled and stuck out his hand, which Clint shook enthusiastically.

"How are you, Clint?"

"I'm fine," Clint said. "What the hell are you doing in Denver?"

"I'm looking for some whores."

7

"What?"

Clint and Weaver had met several years ago when they were invited into the same poker game. They were both finally beaten in the end by Luke Short, but they became friends. Weaver was younger, but Clint and the man got on well, and Clint had followed Weaver's "career" as a gambler ever since. He had, however, recently lost track of the man.

"Have you changed careers?" Clint asked. "No more cards? You running girls now?"

"Not exactly. I can tell you about it if you've got time," Weaver said. "Were you checking in or out?"

"Out, actually," Clint said.

"Was there a game here?"

"No," Clint said, "I was here for one night, passing through."

"So you're not in a hurry to leave?"

"Not really."

"Well, then, stay another night and I'll tell you what I'm involved in. In fact, I have a proposition for you."

Clint turned to the clerk and said, "Looks like I'm staying. Can I get my room back?"

"Of course, Mr. Adams. I'll have your belongings taken back up, if you like."

"Good, thank you." He turned back to his friend and spread his arms. "I'm all yours—and all ears."

"Come on, then," Weaver said, "I'll buy you a drink."

Weaver explained to Clint that he had built and was trying to establish a town in the mountains, taking advantage of a huge gold strike. He was very satisfied with the progress he had made in half a year. Water Hole was starting to have the look and feel of a real town. Although other buildings and businesses had been built and started since he first erected the saloon, he owned the two largest establishments—the Crystal Palace and the mercantile.

Once he established the brothel he decided he'd look into starting a bank. After all, the miners had to have someplace to keep their money for the time in between when they dug it out of the ground and when they passed it over to him. It was a testament—loud and clear—to Weaver's sense of priority that he ranked a bank just behind a brothel.

Still, he thought, how hard would it be to run a bank? But he definitely needed a woman to run the brothel, and he already had the qualifications for the job in mind. She had to be experienced, but not too old, and smart—but not too smart. And it wouldn't hurt if she was beautiful.

To this end, Weaver explained, he was ready to make the ultimate sacrifice and visit Denver's brothels in search of his perfect business partner for this venture.

"So what's your proposition for me?" Clint asked after listening to his friend's tale.

"I want you to come and deal for me."

"Deal what?"

"Whatever you want," Weaver said. "Poker, faro . . . you want to spin the roulette wheel?"

"No," Clint said. "That little white ball makes me dizzy."

"What about dealing?"

Clint thought a moment. It was something he had never done before, and these days that was something that appealed to him. But Weaver was a gambler, and he never did anything without a reason.

"What's the catch, Jed?"

"No catch."

"I know you better than that."

"Maybe you don't."

Clint stared at him a few seconds, then said, "Okay, maybe I don't."

"I have a reason for asking," Weaver said, "but it's not a catch."

"Okay, then, what's the reason?"

"Let me see if I can explain this," Weaver said. "I'm trying to build something, for the first time in my life. Someplace I can live. Someplace other people can live."

"Jed, do you think your town will survive when the strike peters out?"

"It's a huge strike, Clint."

"They all peter out, in the end."

"But maybe this one will last long enough," Weaver said.

"Long enough for . . ."

"For Water Hole to become a real town."

"Water Hole?"

"That's what it's called, for now."

"What good do you think I can do you, Jed?"

"If word gets out that you're dealing in my saloon, people will come."

"Gamblers will come," Clint said. "Are those the people you want to populate your town with?"

"I want everybody there," Weaver said, leaning forward in his chair. "Gamblers, merchants, whores, tradesmen, everybody. What do you say, Clint? You'll be in on the birth of a new town."

"Jed, are you going to stop gambling?"

Weaver sat back.

"No," he said, "I'm not. I'll still be playing poker. Why?"

"Seems to me if you want to be a town builder you shouldn't be a gambler."

"What's more of a gamble than investing everything you've got in a town?"

Clint studied the man across the table. The Jed Weaver he knew was only interested in lining his pockets with other people's money, and the way he did it was to win it. This Jed Weaver—the town builder—was a stranger, but if he was for real, he might turn out to be a better man, a better friend.

"You know what?" Clint said. "I'll give dealing faro a try. Sounds interesting."

TWO

They went out together to hunt for Weaver's madam to run his whorehouse.

"Every town's got to have one," he said. "We've got the saloon, a general store, the whorehouse will be next."

"And then?"

"A bank, a church, more stores, more people," Weaver said, his eyes shining. "A town, Clint!"

It did sound exciting, and it would be interesting to be in on the birth of a town.

But first, the Denver whorehouses.

"Why won't you try a girl?" Weaver asked when they were in a carriage heading for their first stop.

"I've never had to pay for a woman, Jed," Clint said, "and I don't intend to start now."

"But . . . it's research," Weaver reasoned. "We're searching for that perfect woman—"

"—to run the place for you," Clint finished. "You can find her by talking to a bunch of these women, not sleeping with them all."

"Well," Weaver said, "I just consider that a bonus."

"Well, then," Clint said, "you do the research, and I'll do the talking."

13

"See?" Weaver said. "We're operating like a team already."

"Not a team, Jed," Clint said. "I'll be working for you. I don't want to be a partner in this."

"Suit yourself."

When they reached the first place and went inside, Weaver went upstairs with a woman while Clint talked to some of them downstairs. He'd done this sort of thing once before, when a friend of his was trying to outfit a gambling boat with women so he could offer his customers every comfort as they went up and down the Mississippi.

When Jed came down he told Clint he thought he'd found a girl, but not one who could run the place.

"I didn't have much luck either," Clint said. "None of these girls would be smart enough."

"We need someone a little older," Weaver said. "Come on, I know another place."

"How do you know about all these cathouses, Jed?"

"Well, you see," Weaver said, "I don't have your problem about not paying for women. In my life, I've paid for a lot of them."

Her name was Martha Hunt, and she *was* perfect. They found her on the third night. She was thirty-two, about the age where she was too old to be a whore, but a little young to be a madam. She had been in the business since she was seventeen and knew every aspect of it. And she was beautiful, with black hair, white skin, a slender waist that accentuated her already full hips and bust.

Weaver saw her in the fourth establishment he visited. He paid for her time, went upstairs with her, enjoyed her company for an hour or so, and then told her he wanted to talk.

"Whatever you want, honey," she said, "but talkin' is extra."

"That's all right," he said, "I'll pay."

"Do you mind if I smoke while we talk?" she asked. "The old bitch who runs this place won't let us smoke downstairs."

"Of course," Weaver said, although he was surprised when it was a cheroot she lit up and not a cigarette.

"You know," he went on, "if you had your own place you could smoke whenever and wherever you liked."

She laughed derisively. "And what are the chances of that happenin', honey? It takes money to set up a shop like this."

"Well, I've got the money to set it up," he replied, "but I need somebody to run it."

She stared at him, the cigar momentarily forgotten. Weaver watched as tendrils of smoke floated toward the ceiling while he waited for her reaction.

"Is this a joke?"

"It's no joke. I have a town near the California Gulch called Water Hole."

"I never heard of it."

"It's a small town, now," he said. "I only started it six months ago."

"In the mountains?"

He nodded.

"Why would you start a town in the mountains?"

"To be near the miners. That was the whole point."

Her eyes lit up. "Gold miners! That's perfect. A cat-house would do wonderfully there."

"Brothel."

"If you want to get fancy," she said, "why not call it a social club?"

Now it was Weaver's eyes that lit up. "The Water Hole Social Club."

"Water Hole," she said, wrinkling her nose. "Crummy name for a town."

"Maybe," he said, "we'll change it."

"What do I have to do for this opportunity?" she asked suspiciously.

"You have to leave here, recruit some girls, come to Water Hole with me, and set up shop."

"And do I get paid for this?"

"Cash," he said, "or you can have a piece of the action."

"How big a piece?"

He did not think he could get her for the five percent he got Harvey Larch for.

"That's negotiable."

"Well, we've got to negotiate it now," she said, discovering her cheroot again and tasting it. "I'm not about to go into the mountains with a man I just met unless everything is laid out beforehand."

"Well, if that's the case," Weaver said, "I suggest you think over my offer, decide exactly what it is you want, and we'll have dinner tomorrow night to discuss it."

"That's fine," she said, "only I get to pick the place for dinner."

"Of course."

When Weaver came downstairs he found Clint waiting.

"I found her."

"And?"

"We're going to have dinner tomorrow night. She wants to think it over."

"You think she'll take it?"

"I hope so," Weaver said. "She's pretty smart. I'm sure you and I can talk her into it over dinner."

"I'm coming to dinner, too?"

"Well, of course," Weaver said. "You're supposed to be helping me, aren't you?"

"If you say so," Clint replied. "You're the boss."

THREE

They ironed out their "differences" over dinner, which they had in his hotel's dining room. She had specified the Denver House's dining room, and when he told her that's where he and Clint were staying she was impressed.

They met her in the lobby of the hotel and Weaver introduced her to Clint, who was immediately impressed by her appearance. She was wearing a blue dress, worn off the shoulder and cut very low in front to exhibit what seemed like acres of creamy cleavage.

They went into the dining room and ordered dinner. They discussed exactly what her job would be, and what her cut would be, and then Weaver announced it was time for her to make up her mind.

"So that's all there is to it?" she asked.

"Except for one other thing."

"And what's that?"

"You have to be ready, with six girls, to leave by day after tomorrow."

"Only six? In two days?"

"That should be enough for a start."

"You're lucky I know some girls who won't mind making a change."

17

"They won't mind leaving Denver for a small mining town?"

"With potential, you said."

"Yes."

She shook her head. "As long as the terms are right, they'll move."

"That will be between you and them."

"And you're certain that this town of yours, this Water hole"—she said it with a face—"is going to prosper?"

"I'm betting everything I have on it."

"Well," she said, "I can do that, too, since I ain't got much." She turned to Clint. "What about you, Clint? You've been quiet."

"Jed was doing so well," Clint said, "I didn't want to get in the way."

"What's your cut here?"

"No cut," he said. "I'm just the faro dealer."

She gave him a look and said, "I've heard of you, you know. You're not just a faro dealer."

"Actually," Clint said, "I've never been a faro dealer. This is going to be my first time, and I'm excited about it."

"So . . . you're not a partner in this venture?"

"Clint's a friend, and he's agreed to help me with the gambling operation in my saloon. That's all."

He poured her a glass of champagne, one for himself, and one for Clint, then raised his in a toast.

"To us, and the Water Hole Social Club."

She clinked glasses with him and said, "We've got to do something about that name—and speaking of names?"

"What about them?"

"I'd like to change mine."

"Why?" Clint asked.

She made a face. "I never have liked Martha. I want to think of something more appropriate for a madam."

"You can call yourself anything you like," Weaver said.

"Let me think about it."

They finished their champagne, then had some pie and coffee.

"Well," Weaver said, "I'm going to turn in."

"Is that a hint?" she asked.

"What?" Weaver asked.

"There's one other thing I should tell you," she said.

"What's that?"

"I don't sleep with people I work for. It gets in the way of business."

"That's not part of the deal," he told her. "You sleep with who you want to sleep with."

"Good," Martha said. "Then we won't have a problem."

"Clint? Would you see that Martha gets safely to a cab?"

"It would be my pleasure."

Weaver stood up. "Then I'll say good night. I'll see you both tomorrow."

Both Clint and Martha remained quiet until Weaver had left the dining room.

"Would you like anything else?" Clint asked.

"Yes," she said. "I've never been in this hotel before tonight. Before I leave Denver I would like to see one of the rooms."

"Well," Clint said, "I think that can be arranged."

He waved to their waiter.

FOUR

Two days later they left Denver with six girls in a buckboard, Weaver leading the way on his horse, Clint trailing on Duke. Luckily, Martha—who was now calling herself Danielle, for some reason—and one of the other girls knew how to drive a team, and could take turns. Still, it wasn't an easy journey ten thousand feet up the mountain with a buckboard. They suffered a broken wheel, and when it snapped one of the girls was pitched off the wagon and broke her arm. By the time they arrived in Water Hole the girls were dirty and in bad tempers—which didn't matter much to the miners, who were in favor of plucking them right off the buckboard for some fun. Weaver and Clint had to stand them off—Weaver with gun in hand, even though everybody knew he wouldn't shoot any of them—probably.

"Just settle down, boys," Weaver shouted, standing in his stirrups, getting his horse between the bulk of the crowd and the buckboard of women. "These ladies have come a long way to get here and gone through a lot. Least you could do is give them time to rest up, get cleaned up and all pretty smelling for you."

"How long will that take?" someone shouted, and everyone laughed.

"At least a few hours," Weaver replied. "Give 'em that long and then come and see them at the newly opened Water Hole Social Club."

"Where's that?"

Weaver frowned. It occurred to him that he didn't know where Quinn had erected the building in his absence.

"Can't say for sure, right now," he admitted, "but come by the Crystal Palace and we'll give you directions. In fact, why don't you all go on over there now and have a beer on me."

A free drink did more to disperse the crowd than a gun ever could have.

Weaver holstered his gun and turned to look at the seven disheveled ladies who truly did, at that moment, look like soiled doves.

"A few hours?" Martha/Danielle said. "That's all the rest my girls get?"

"Long enough for a bath and a change of clothes," Weaver said. "This is a gold town, Martha—"

"Danielle."

"Danielle," he corrected himself, "and these boys have gold dust burning holes in their pockets. We have to get it while the gettin' is good."

"What about Angela?" Danielle asked. "She can't work with a broken arm, and she probably needs lookin' at."

"I'll bring a doctor—or the closest thing we have to one—over to the social club to see to her . . . as soon as we find out where the damned place is!"

Weaver had a few rooms upstairs from his saloon to rent out, and he gave one to Clint, his new faro dealer.

"This is impressive, Jed," Clint said, looking around the Crystal Palace.

"Get yourself settled upstairs and then come down and

have a drink," Weaver said. "I'll introduce you to everyone else."

"Okay," Clint said.

"First three doors are empty rooms," Weaver said.
"Take whichever one you like."

Clint went up the stairs, but instead of checking out
all three rooms and choosing one he simply went into
the first one. It was small but clean, and it smelled of
new wood. He dropped his belongings into a corner for
the time being and sat on the bed. The mattress seemed
decent enough. Of course, it wasn't as plush as the mattress in his hotel room in Denver, the one he and Martha—now Danielle—had given a real workout that first
night.

As soon as they entered the room Martha didn't make
any pretense about looking it over. She turned and came
into Clint's arms eagerly, anxiously. They kissed for a
long time before she pulled her mouth away and looked
into his eyes.

"Do you find this strange?" she asked.

"Do I find what strange?"

"That a whore would be this . . . enthusiastic about
sex?"

"No," he said.

"Why not?"

"Because that's your job," he said, "and this is for
pleasure."

"It sure is," she said, and kissed him again before
backing away and starting to remove her clothes.

Clint hurried to keep up with her and got his own
clothes off in record time. They fell onto the bed locked
in an embrace which seemed to fuse them together. His
skin was so hot it seemed to warm him completely. His
hard penis was trapped between them, her breasts full
and cushiony against his chest. She was a full-bodied
woman, with good hips and a well-padded butt, and Clint

ran his hands all over her, and then his mouth. She moaned as his lips and tongue explored her, kissing and licking her breasts and nipples, taking as much of her breasts into his mouth as he could and then continuing down over her convex belly until his mouth was pressed between her legs and his tongue was working avidly.

"Oooh, oooh," she moaned, pressing herself into his face, lifting her buttocks from the bed, "yes, yes, oohh, like that, right there, oh, God . . ."

It didn't take long before she went over the edge, and then he mounted her and slid right into her because she was so wet. As hot as her skin was, inside she was hotter still. He slid his hands beneath her to cup her buttocks, and as she exhorted him to fuck her harder, harder, he fell into a mindless tempo where he sought nothing but his own satisfaction, banging into her as hard as she wanted, and harder still, the bed bouncing on the floor, the bedpost knocking against the wall until finally he exploded inside of her. . . .

He stared down at the bed in his room at the Crystal Palace and knew that it would never stand up to that kind of treatment. They'd probably knock down the wall or cave in the floor, as well. Of course, he didn't know if there'd be a repeat of that performance now that they were in Water Hole and "Danielle" was working. He'd just have to wait and see.

FIVE

Downstairs Jed Weaver checked in with his right hand, Ollie Quinn. Quinn was an intense, dark man with craggy features. He had the blackest eyebrows Weaver had ever seen on a man, above the bluest eyes—cold eyes that never left your face while he was speaking with you.

When Weaver entered his office Quinn was there, sitting in the chair in front of Weaver's desk.

"Why aren't you at the desk?" he asked.

"I never sit at your desk."

Quinn stood up and shook hands with his friend and boss. His hair was slicked back, and he smelled recently barbered.

"How was the trip?"

"It went great," Weaver said, moving around to sit at his desk.

"Found the woman you wanted?"

"The woman, the girls, and a surprise."

Quinn sat back down.

"What's the surprise?"

"Clint Adams."

"The Gunsmith?"

"That's right."

"Why is he a surprise?"

"I ran into him in Denver, at the Denver House."

"He stays there when he's in town, same as you," Quinn said. "I'm surprised you never ran into him there before."

"Well, it's a good thing I ran into him this time."

"Why?"

"Because he's agreed to come here and deal faro."

"He's coming here?"

"He's here, in a room upstairs right now."

"I didn't know he dealt faro."

"He didn't, until now."

Quinn was frowning, and Weaver noticed.

"What is it? Oh, I know, you're supposed to hire the dealers—"

"That's not it."

"What, then?"

"His reputation."

"What about it?"

"It's going to attract the wrong crowd."

"It's going to attract a crowd," Weaver said, changing the statement subtly. "That's what I want."

"There'll be trouble, Jed."

"We'll handle it," Weaver said. "Clint'll handle it, and so will you. I want you to meet him."

"I guess I'd better," Quinn said, "if we're going to be handling trouble together."

"Come on, Ollie, relax," Weaver said. "This is gonna be good for us. You'll see."

"Yeah," Quinn said, still unconvinced, "I'll wait and see."

"All right, then," Weaver said, sitting back in his chair, "tell me what went on while I was gone. . . ."

SIX

Clint came downstairs and saw that the place had started to fill up just during the time he was checking out his room. He knew that when the miners came up for air it would get busier still.

He walked to the bar and ordered a beer.

"No charge," the bartender said. "You're Adams, right?"

"Right."

"Boss told me you're workin' here now. I never knew you were a faro dealer."

"It's a new career for me," Clint said, accepting the beer.

"My name's Leo," the man said, "head bartender."

"How many bartenders are there?" Clint asked, accepting the proffered hand, which was callused on the palm and showed signs on the knuckles, which were smashed flat, of the man having once been a fighter. He must have been a pretty good fighter, though, because his face wasn't too marked up.

"Three."

"How long ago did you quit fighting?" Clint asked.

"A few years," Leo said. "You're observant."

"Only one way your knuckles get like that."

"I was pretty good," Leo said. Then he touched his face and added, "Good enough to stay pretty, huh?"

He wasn't pretty, but his face didn't look like an old fighter's—maybe like a old bartender's, though. The scars he did have could have come from bar fights, and the red in his nose came from sampling the stock.

"To tell the truth I started drinking and that was the end of my ring career," Leo said. "Mr. Weaver, he sort of saved my life by giving me this job. Course, he told me if he ever finds me drunk he'll fire me."

"Tough way to stop drinking," Clint said.

"Well, it's worked, so far. 'Scuse me."

Leo went down the bar to wait on some early miners. Clint turned his back, leaned against the bar, and sipped his beer while taking the place in. A door opened in the back and out stepped Weaver and another man with slicked back, dark hair and the blackest eyebrows Clint had ever seen. When Weaver saw him he said something to the other man and they both came toward him.

"I see you met Leo," Weaver said, "and found out you can drink for free."

"A fringe benefit you didn't tell me about when you offered me the job," Clint said.

"There are others, too," Weaver said. "Clint, I want you to meet Ollie Quinn. Ollie, Clint Adams."

"I've heard a lot about you," Clint said to Quinn. Weaver had explained who Quinn was during the ride up the mountain.

"I know you by reputation only."

Weaver looked on as the two men sized each other up.

"Quinn is my right hand," he said. "He also hires the dealers, and overlooks security."

"Guess I'm working for you, then," Clint said.

"Hardly," Quinn said. "I realize you're friends with Jed and you're probably just doing this as a favor."

"It'll be a new experience for me," Clint said. "That's basically why I'm doing it."

"Well, we'll set you up at a table and I'll introduce you to some of the others. Excuse me, I have some things to take care of. It was nice meeting you."

Clint watched as Quinn walked off and disappeared through a doorway.

"He's not thrilled that I'm here," he said.

"He'll come around," Weaver said.

"What's his problem? That he didn't get to hire me?"

"He thinks you'll attract the wrong kind of people."

"That's right," Clint said, "you said he was security. Well, he may have a point."

"If there's any trouble I'm sure you and Quinn can handle it."

"Maybe Quinn won't want my help."

"It'll work out," Weaver said. "Wait and see. Come on, I'll show you where your table is."

SEVEN

Clint got set up at his faro table. He'd played faro for years, although he didn't like it as much as poker. Wyatt Earp was possibly the best dealer he'd ever seen, and he'd watched him work many times. He also knew when people heard that he was dealing they'd come in just to see if they could beat him.

He met some of the other dealers who, he thought, regarded him oddly. They knew his reputation and probably wondered what he was doing here as a faro dealer.

He hoped he wouldn't have any trouble being accepted by the others, but Quinn was the one he really didn't want to be at odds with. Weaver had explained that he and Quinn were friends, and that the man was fiercely loyal to him. He'd go along with Weaver's decision to have Clint deal faro, but that didn't mean he'd like the idea—or Clint. For Weaver's sake, he hoped that he and Quinn would get along.

He dealt for the first time that night and did fairly well. He'd been on the other side of the table many times; it would take some getting used to, being on the opposite side for a change.

He had no relief dealer. When he wanted to take a

31

break he simply closed the table. He'd learned this from
Wyatt Earp, who would let no one touch his cards or his
table.

When he took a break he went to the bar and had a
beer. He never drank when he played poker, so he kept
to the same philosophy when he was dealing faro.

On the first night, while he was on a break at the bar
he got a chance to see Ollie Quinn in action. Quinn had
a man with a shotgun on a platform in the rear of the
saloon, but that man was not there to handle altercations
between customers, he was there in case somebody tried
to hold the place up. That was the only situation in which
the man would cut loose with both barrels of his scatter-
gun.

Quinn was a constant presence in the saloon when it
became busy. It was filled with miners, grifters, gamblers,
merchants, and travelers, who were all interested in one
thing—gold. The miners dug it out of the ground and
then came into town, where everyone else tried to get it
from them. Quinn kept a wary eye on all this, because
the lust for gold dust was sure to cause trouble.

On this night the trouble came from one of the poker
tables. To avoid the onus of cheating falling over any of
the tables, Weaver had house dealers working the poker
tables. The only cards the players got their hands on were
their own—or the ones they had hidden up their sleeves.

Clint wasn't watching any table in particular, but he
noticed Quinn moving across the floor, his intense eyes
riveted to one table. As the man reached the poker table,
one of the players stood up and shouted, ''Goddamn it,
that's the last time—'' while going for his gun. Before
he could clear leather, though, Quinn's right hand came
down on the man's gun hand, pinning it to the gun and
the gun in the holster. With his left hand he grabbed the
back of the man's belt.

''What the—'' the man said, but before he realized

what was happening Quinn was walking him to the front door, and outside.

Clint walked to the door and looked outside. Quinn and the irate man were standing in the street and the man was pleading his case. Quinn listened, then spoke briefly to the man. He turned then, leaving the man in the street, and started to walk away. Clint saw the man go for his gun and was about to step outside when Quinn turned quickly, as if he had eyes in the back of his head. As the man came up with his gun, Quinn caught hold of his arm and Clint heard the sound as the man's arm broke with an audible crack. A look of shock and pain crossed the man's face as he went to his knees. Quinn kept the man's gun, tucked it into his belt, and left him on his knees in the street, cradling his broken arm.

Quinn entered the saloon and saw Clint standing there.

"I thought you might need some help," Clint said.

"Not usually," Quinn said, "but thanks." The last was said grudgingly.

"I admire the way you got him out of here without any trouble."

"Better to get them outside quick. There's too many people could get hurt in here."

"I realize that."

"I've got to get back to work."

"Yeah," Clint said, "so do I."

Quinn moved back into the crowded saloon. Clint went to the bar, left the empty mug there, and walked back to his table.

That was the first night on the job.

EIGHT

A couple of boardinghouses had opened up around town, but Water Hole needed a hotel and a bank. In the same single-minded fashion which he had used to establish his Crystal Palace, his mercantile, and his social club, Weaver saw to it that the next few months gave birth to the Water Hole Hotel and the Bank of Water Hole. The bank didn't have a safe. That was not the kind of thing that was easily transportable over ten thousand feet of mountains. So they constructed a room to house the money, and lined the walls with shelves. Two armed guards stood in front of the room day and night, and there were no windows or doors other than the one.

Water Hole, with a saloon, a mercantile, a whorehouse, a hotel, and a bank was still not a full-fledged town. Father O'Shay had come to town and established a church. Some of the miners brought their families in, and a school was constructed. The town now housed merchants, miners, speculators, gamblers, prostitutes, and bandits. They also named a sheriff, and a mayor—who turned out to be Jed Weaver. The sheriff was Ollie Quinn. Before long California Gulch was home to more than ten thousand people, and many of them lived, worked, or gambled in the town of Water Hole, and spent money every day in an establishment that was owned by Jed Weaver.

Most of the businesses in Water Hole were owned by Weaver—whose gamble seemed to be paying off nicely— they were dependent on him, as well.

By the end of the month Clint was as good a faro dealer as he was ever going to be—not in the same league with Wyatt Earp, but good enough. Weaver's gamble here seemed to be paying off, as well. Men were coming into Water Hole, and into the Crystal Palace, just to play at the Gunsmith's faro table.

Clint enjoyed being in on the birth of a town, as Weaver had suggested he might. He became fairly well known, and had even been offered the sheriff's job before it was given to Ollie Quinn. That was something that Quinn did not appreciate.

That was the one thing that had not gone as well as Clint had hoped—his relationship with Ollie Quinn. Despite his efforts to the contrary, it had become something of a competitive and adversarial relationship. Clint being offered the sheriff's job first hadn't helped matters. He met with Weaver in his office one night to discuss it.

"I think we may have a problem," Clint said.

"Have a seat," Weaver replied. "What's the problem?"

"Quinn."

"What about him?"

"He doesn't like me."

"You can't be liked by everybody, Clint."

"But it goes deeper than that," Clint said. "I think he resents me."

"Quinn? He hasn't got a resentful bone in his body."

"Then this must be a recent development," Clint said. "I think I should leave, Jed."

"Whoa, wait a minute," Weaver said, sitting forward. "Are you tired of dealing?"

"Well, no, but—"

"But nothin'," Weaver said. "You're bringin' in a lot of business, Clint. Do you want a bigger cut?"

"No," Clint said, "the money's fine, and I'm still enjoying what I'm doing."

"Well, then, stick it out," Weaver said. "I'll talk to Quinn if you like."

"No," Clint said quickly, "that'd be the worse thing you could do. It would only make matters worse."

"Then what would make them better, other than you leaving?"

"I don't know," Clint said. "I'm trying my best to get along with him, but when you offered me the job of sheriff that just made it worse."

"I just thought you were the best man for the job."

"So when you offered it to him," Clint said, "it made him second best in your eyes."

"That's not the way I meant it at all."

"But that's the way it came off."

Weaver sat back and thought a moment.

"Let me ask you something."

"What?"

"What's your relationship with Danielle?"

"Why is that—"

"Did you and she sleep together in Denver?" Weaver asked. "I think this is important."

"Well, yes, that first night—"

"And since you've been here?"

"A couple more times the first week, but not since then," Clint said.

"Why not?"

"I guess we've just been too busy doing our own jobs," Clint said. "What's this about?"

"Quinn goes over to the social club very often."

"So?"

"He doesn't go there to see any of the girls."

It took Clint a moment to catch on, and then he said, "Oh, I think I see."

Weaver nodded.

"He and Danielle seem to be getting along real well," he said. "They have time for each other."

"Well, maybe she didn't tell him about her and me."

"If she did," Weaver said, "or if she ever does, it will play right into this business of him feeling like he's second choice."

"It sure will."

"Well," Weaver said, "maybe that won't happen. I mean, why would she tell him?"

"I don't know," Clint said. "I can't predict what a woman will do, or why."

"I know what you mean."

"All right," Clint said, standing, "I'll try to stick out a few more weeks and see what happens."

"Thanks, Clint," Weaver said, "I appreciate it. I'd hate to have to choose between you and Quinn."

Clint frowned.

"You'd choose Quinn, naturally."

"I'm not so sure," Weaver said. "You bring in a lot of business."

"You need Quinn, Jed," Clint said. "I *would* leave before I'd make you choose between us."

"Well," Weaver said, "maybe it won't come to that, but if it did I'd have to make a business decision, Clint."

Weaver turned his attention to the paperwork on his desk and Clint left, frowning. Something about Weaver was beginning to change, and Clint wasn't sure he liked it.

NINE

Ollie Quinn rolled over in bed and put his hand on Danielle's bare back. He ran his palm down the line of her back until it was resting on her bare butt.

"Mmmm," she said, "just rub me there."

He began to move his hand in a circular motion over her butt, massaging both cheeks, enjoying the way her smooth skin felt beneath his hand.

"Ollie?"

"Hmm?"

"Can I ask you a question?"

"Sure, Martha." He was the only one who still called her that, because it was her real name.

"Are you getting serious about me?"

"That depends on what you mean by serious."

"I mean," she said, without lifting her head, which was resting on her arms, "are you thinking about marriage and babies and a picket fence?"

"If that's your definition of serious," he said, "then the answer is no."

She remained silent.

"But my definition of serious," he went on, running his finger along the smooth cleft between her butt cheeks,

39

"is when you can't imagine yourself ever going through one day without seeing a person."

"And by that definition," she asked, "are you getting serious about me?"

"No," he said, then quickly added, "I'm not *getting* serious about you because I'm *already* serious about you."

"Well, then," she said, "by your definition, I guess I'm serious about you, too."

"That's good," he said. He leaned over her and replaced his finger with his lips, and his tongue.

"Mmmmm," she murmured, moving her butt around as he kissed it. "So what are we going to do about it?"

"About what?"

"About the fact that we're serious about each other?"

"Why do we have to do anything?" he asked.

Abruptly, she rolled over and looked at him. He stared at her firm breasts, loving every freckle and vein that he could see.

"Come on, Ollie," she said, "how long is this place going to last?"

"What do you mean by 'this place'?" he asked.

"I mean this town," she said, "Water Hole. It's a gold town, you know they don't last long."

"Jed's plan," Quinn said, "is for this town to last long after the gold is gone, Martha."

"Well, how realistic do you think that plan is?"

"I think it's very realistic."

"Do you really?"

"I was with Jed when he came up with this plan, Martha," he reminded her. "He's gonna make it work."

"Do you really think so?"

"I do."

She sat up and put both of her hands on his arms. She loved his biceps because they were like rocks.

"Will you promise me something?"

"Sure."

"At the first sign of trouble," she said, "the first sign that things are going wrong, will you tell me?"

"Things aren't going to go wrong, Martha—"

"Just promise me, then," she said, "so I'll feel better. You don't even have to believe it."

"All right, then," he said. "I promise."

She leaned into him, pressing her cheek to his chest, and his arms went around her.

"Thank you, Ollie," she said. "I just have to know that you'll be looking out for us."

"I'll always be looking out for us, Martha," he said, holding her tightly. "You don't ever have to worry about that."

TEN

Angela Tompkins was the girl who had been pitched off the wagon when the wheel snapped. It had taken a month for the arm to heal sufficiently for her to work. Clint came by for that month to see how she was, and they became friends. For that reason when she wasn't working she would come by his room sometimes. She never charged him.

Water Hole didn't have a proper doctor yet, but they had a man who had set more broken bones than most doctors had. He owned the livery stable—with Jed Weaver—but whenever there was doctoring to be done, people went to Willy Mack. Willy had set Angela's arm, and he had set it properly. It healed cleanly, and she was grateful for that. So was Clint, who watched her sleeping beside him now, that arm across her forehead.

Angela was a blonde, her hair the color of wheat. She had very light eyebrows, and the sun coming in the windows made the down on her arms glow. She was tall and slender, small-breasted and long-legged, and very passionate in bed when she wasn't working. When she was working, she told Clint, she was very good at her job, but passion never entered into her "performance."

Not like with him.

43

She woke now and stared up at him, smiling. She had a very unusual upper lip that was very expressive and mobile. It fascinated him that it never seemed to move the same way twice in a row.

"How long have you been watching me?"

"Not long."

"Why are you watching me?"

"Because you're beautiful."

"I'm not," she said.

"You are."

"Some of the others are more beautiful," she said. "Elizabeth, now she's beautiful. And Portia."

"With a name like that she'd have to be," he said, and they both laughed.

"And Danielle," she said, "she's beautiful, too."

"Yes, she is."

"Why aren't you with one of them?"

"They don't interest me like you do."

"So I'm more interesting than they are?"

"That's right."

"Meaning we can talk?"

"Yes."

She reached up and stroked his face.

"I thought, when we first came here, that you and Danielle—Martha—were . . ."

"Once or twice," he said, "but that was it."

"She's with Quinn now."

"I know."

She shivered and rubbed her arms.

"He scares me."

"Why?"

"Because he looks right through me," she said. "The rest of the girls feel the same way. He doesn't see us."

"I wonder why that is?"

"I think it's because of what we do," she said. "He doesn't approve."

"What about Danielle?" Clint asked. "Does he approve of her?"

"She doesn't go with the customers," Angela said. "We do."

"But she's in charge."

"Still," she said, "he wouldn't touch any of us. He made that clear the first time he came in."

"What else do you know about Quinn?" Clint asked.

"Something I'll bet you don't know."

"What's that?"

"He goes to church."

Clint was surprised.

"You're right," he said. "I didn't know that."

"He's a religious man."

"And he works in a saloon?"

"He's also an odd man," she said. "That's why he scares us. I've always found religious men to be unpredictable."

"I guess you're right, Angela. There's more to Quinn than meets the eye."

"He doesn't like you."

"Now that I do know."

"Why?"

"I think he feels threatened by me."

"Do you want his job?"

"No, but he's threatened anyway."

"He's dangerous."

"Yes, I think he is."

"But so are you."

"Sometimes."

She put her hand on his chest and said, "But not with me."

"No," he said, "not with you, not ever."

Her hand traveled lower and she began to stroke him. He grew in her hand.

"Lie back," she said, pushing him gently. "I want to say good morning."

He did as she said, and she said good morning sweetly, first with her mouth, and then mounting him and sliding him into her.

"Oooh, yes," she said, sitting astride him, "this is the way to say good morning."

"Amen," he said.

ELEVEN

Later, at breakfast, Clint thought about what he'd learned about Quinn. The man had never struck him as being religious, and if he was, what was he doing working for a gambler and consorting with a whore? Apparently, he was very selective about his religious beliefs.

The Crystal Palace wasn't open yet so Clint had the place to himself until some of the other employees came down for breakfast. He had left Angela fast asleep in his bed after they'd said good morning vigorously.

"Here's your breakfast, Clint," Leo said. He was not only the head bartender, but the cook, as well—at least, in the morning. He set a plate of eggs and bacon in front of him, and a basket of biscuits.

"Leo, I swear," Clint said, "you make the best biscuits I've ever had."

"Used to cook with my mother when I was a kid," Leo said. "You don't forget. Another pot of coffee?"

"Definitely," Clint said. The bartender also made excellent coffee.

While Clint was eating his breakfast and waiting for the second pot of coffee, Quinn came down the stairs. As usual he was impeccably dressed in a black suit and a white boiled shirt, with a black string tie. He stopped

47

when he got to the bottom of the stairs and realized no one else was up but Clint.

"Good morning, Quinn," Clint said.

"Morning."

"Join me for breakfast," Clint said. "Leo is outdoing himself this morning."

Quinn hesitated, as if trying to think of a way out, but then he shrugged and came over to the table.

"Haven't seen Jed this morning," Clint said.

"Big game," Quinn said. "He's not usually down early after a big game."

Clint knew about Jed Weaver's big games. In fact, Weaver had invited him to participate and he'd declined.

"You're turning down a big game?" Weaver had asked.

"I work for you, Jed," Clint had said, "I'm not going to be seen playing in a big game against you. It wouldn't be good for you."

"Why don't you let me be the judge of what's good for me?"

"No," Clint said, "I'm going to help you out this time."

So Clint didn't play, and he decided not to let Quinn know that he'd been invited.

"How's his luck running?" Clint asked.

"As always," Quinn said, "good."

At that point Leo came out with the second pot of coffee, and a cup for Quinn.

"Thought I heard you out here, Mr. Quinn. The usual today?"

"Yes, Leo, thanks."

Leo poured them each a cup of coffee and went off to get Quinn's steak and eggs, which he ate every morning.

"How are you liking it here, Adams?" he asked.

Clint was surprised by the question.

"I like it fine, Quinn. I'm enjoying the dealing."

"Well," Quinn said, "that's good." Clint knew Quinn didn't think it was good, at all.

"How long do you intend to stay?"

"Not permanently, if that's what you're worried about, Quinn," Clint said. "A little longer, perhaps, but not for good."

In fact, Clint had already stayed in one place longer than he usually did, and was surprised that he didn't have the urge to move on yet. He truly was enjoying the dealing, though, and the competition, and—truth be told—so far was enjoying being an attraction for Weaver. On top of everything else, no one had tried anything with him yet, and that was also a surprise.

"I'll bet you thought there would have been a lot of trouble by now," Clint said.

"You're right," Quinn said, "I did. I still do."

"You'd like me to leave."

Quinn shrugged and drank his coffee.

"Come on, Quinn," Clint said. "Since I first came here you haven't liked me. What did I do to you?"

"Nothing."

"Then why do you dislike me so?"

"I just do," Quinn answered. "I don't know that I can put it into words any better than that."

"Well," Clint said, "that's honest."

"Now you be honest," Quinn said.

"About what?"

"You don't like me, either, do you?"

"Actually," Clint said, "when I got here I thought we could be friends."

"And now you don't like me."

"No, that's not true," Clint said. "I don't dislike you. I get the feeling you think I'm after your job."

"You couldn't get my job."

"I don't want it, Quinn."

Quinn just stared at him, and Clint knew what Angela meant by the man looking right through you.

At that point Leo came out with Quinn's steak and eggs. The steak looked as if it had hardly spent any time on the fire. The plate was running with blood, which colored the eggs. Quinn picked up his knife and fork and started eating, and the two men finished their breakfast in silence.

TWELVE

The awkward breakfast ended when Quinn pushed away from the table, got up, and left. Clint decided he'd made his last overture to the man. If Quinn had a problem with him, let him deal with it himself. Clint was having too much fun dealing faro and watching Weaver build his town.

Clint was finishing up when Weaver came down from his room.

"Coffee, Leo!" he shouted.

"Comin' up, boss."

"Morning," Clint greeted.

"Good morning," Weaver said, but he was scowling.

"How's the game going?"

Weaver didn't look at him when he answered.

"Some minor setbacks, but it'll change," he said.

"Bad hands?"

"Good hands," Weaver said, "but I'm running into better."

"It'll turn around."

Weaver looked at Clint for the first time and said, "It always does."

Clint was surprised at Weaver's appearance. The man had dark circles beneath his eyes and looked haggard.

51

Leo came out with the coffee and asked, "Breakfast, boss?"

"Not today."

"You gotta eat something."

"I'll make it up at lunch."

Leo looked like he was going to say something else, then thought better of it.

"More coffee, Mr. Adams?"

"I'm floating now, Leo, thanks."

The ex-fighter turned bartender shrugged and went back to the kitchen.

"You hurt his feelings," Clint said.

"What?"

"He wants to cook for you."

Weaver scowled. "I don't eat breakfast when I'm losing."

"How bad?"

"Bad enough," Weaver said, "but like I said, it'll turn around. Seen Quinn this morning?"

"We had breakfast together . . . sort of."

"You makin' friends?"

"We ate at the same table," Clint said, "but we didn't talk much."

"You two should get along better."

"I tried, Jed. I'm through trying. From now on let him try."

Weaver drank half his coffee and put the cup down, shoving back his chair.

"Where are you going?" Clint asked.

"I've got to see a man about a telegraph line."

"All the way up here?"

"Maybe."

"That's a lot of wire."

"It's just something we're gonna talk about."

"When's your game start up again?"

"Noon. Change your mind about playing?"

"No."

"I wish you would," Weaver said. "Another player in the game might change my luck."

"Sorry."

"Well," Weaver said, "come and sit in whenever the urge hits you. The others in the game keep askin' if you're gonna play."

"Send them out to play faro."

Weaver laughed and said, "There's not a faro player in the bunch."

"Maybe I can convert them."

"I'll put it to them. See you later."

"Good luck with your wire."

Weaver waved a hand behind him as he went out the door.

THIRTEEN

Angela came down as Clint was getting ready to leave the saloon and he walked her to the social club. Danielle was out front as Angela kissed Clint and went inside.

"Hello, Ma—Danielle," Clint said. He still forgot her name change sometimes.

"You and Angela are getting along pretty good," she said.

"She's a nice girl."

"She's a whore, like the others."

He detected a note of jealousy, and thought it odd, considering they had only been together a couple of times, and it seemed a mutual decision not to continue. Also, she was with Quinn now.

"That's kind of harsh," Clint said, "considering the same could be said of you now."

"Not anymore," she said. "I'm not a whore anymore, I just run them."

Clint decided not to argue with her, especially since she seemed to want to argue, for some reason.

"Look," she said suddenly, "I'm sorry, I don't want to fight."

"What's wrong, Danielle?"

"I'm . . . getting nervous."

"About what?"

"About this town, and how long it's going to last."

"Have you heard something from the miners who come to your place?"

"No, nothing, but if the mines were petering out would they talk about it?"

"Sure they would."

"Then I guess I'll keep my ears open," she said. "Thanks."

"Don't mention it."

"I'm sorry about what I said. You're right, Angela is a nice kid."

She went inside and Clint wondered if she had voiced her concerns to Quinn. Or if Quinn had said something to her that made her nervous. As far as he knew everything was fine. The mines were still producing, and the miners were still bringing their gold into town to either spend it or lose it.

He decided that he'd keep his ears open, as well.

That night while he was dealing he was careful to listen to the conversations going on around him, both while he was working, and while he was having a beer at the bar during a break.

The place was as rowdy as usual. Quinn had walked a couple of men outside before they could get out of hand, and hadn't broken any bones while doing it. Clint was doing well at his table. One of the miners whooped and hollered when his number came up on the roulette wheel, but he was quick to let it ride and lost it right back again.

Weaver was in the back room where all of his private games were played and Clint hadn't heard anything from there. There was a replacement bartender behind the bar—a young man named Eddie—while Leo took drink orders to the private game.

One thing Clint had found odd about the Crystal Palace was that Weaver hadn't hired any girls to work the place.

"The girls are at the social club," he'd explained once. "The men come here to gamble."

Still, most saloons had girls working the floor, even if it was just to bring drinks to the tables. However, Clint wasn't about to tell Weaver how to run his saloon, or his town.

Clint went back to work at his table and, about half an hour later, didn't know why he looked up, but he did. At that moment a man came through the bat-wing doors and he recognized him immediately. The man looked around the place, spotted Clint, and came walking over.

"Boys," Clint said to the players fanned out in front of him, "I've got to close for a short while. Come back later."

"Come back to visit our money, you mean," one man said, as they all faded away and made room for the new man.

"I heard about it, but I didn't believe it," Luke Short said.

"Luke," Clint said, sticking out his hand, "how the hell are you?"

"Surprised as hell," Short said. He was a small, wiry man dressed like a dandy, but Clint knew no one was less a dandy than Luke Short. "What the hell are you doing dealing faro?"

"I got the offer and decided to take it," Clint said. "It's a new experience for me."

"Are you any better at it than you are at poker?" Short joked.

"That was a fluke," Clint said, referring to the last game they had played in, which Short had won. It wasn't, though, because they both knew that Short was the better poker player of the two—maybe the best poker player Clint knew, although his friend Bat Masterson would argue that one.

"Care to try me?"

Short spread his hands and backed up a pace.

"Faro's not my game," Short said, "and far be it from me to play another man's game."

"You always were a smart gambler."

Short looked around the Crystal Palace, then back at Clint.

"So tell me, who made you the offer that got you behind the faro table?" he asked. "Whose place is this?"

"Jedediah Weaver."

"I know him."

"Yeah, you do. We played with him a couple of times."

"He was pretty good."

"And he's gotten better."

"Is he still playing now that he owns the joint?"

Clint nodded. "In fact, he's got a high-stakes private game going right now, and he's looking for another player to sit in and change the flow of the cards."

"Well," Short said, "I came here to see you, but I wouldn't refuse a game."

"I'll get you in, if you like."

"Won't the other players object, if they've been playing awhile?"

"Who would object to playing poker with you, Luke?"

Short smiled and said, "Just about anybody who ever played with me before."

FOURTEEN

When Weaver heard that Luke Short was in his place, he came charging out of the back room. He welcomed a new player in the game, hoping that it would change the flow of the cards, but he also welcomed the chance to play against Luke Short again.

"Luke, it's good to see you," Weaver said, shaking Short's hand.

"And you, Jed. Seems you've done well for yourself."

"I'm doing okay."

"Well, you got Clint Adams to deal faro for you. That must have took some talking."

"I can be persuasive when I want to be, Luke."

"Well, hopefully so can Clint. He says he can get me into your game."

"Say no more," Weaver said. "You're in. Where are you staying?"

"I haven't checked into a hotel or rooming house yet."

"Then don't. I have a room upstairs you can stay in."

"That's kind of you, Jed."

"Would you like to freshen up before you join the game?"

"That would be nice."

59

"I'll take you up to the room myself," Weaver said. "Come with me."

"Clint," Short said, "we'll catch up later."

"I'll be around, Luke."

Weaver allowed Short to precede him, then turned and mouthed, "Thank you," at Clint, who took it more as, "Thank *you*!"

Clint wondered if, with his luck going bad, Weaver would really be thanking him later for getting Luke Short into the game.

Weaver showed Short to his room and then said, "Come on down when you're ready and Clint can bring you into the back room."

"I'll be along in a little while," Short promised.

Weaver stepped out into the hall and closed the door to Luke Short's room. Getting another player at the table should be enough to turn his luck, but having a player of Short's caliber in the game was dangerous. Still, Jedediah Weaver was never one to back down from a challenge. His luck with the cards hadn't exactly been bad. So far he'd lost twice with a full house to a better full house, and a royal flush, and once he'd had four jacks only to lose to four kings. The cards were coming, but he was getting beat by better hands—and he was losing a lot of money because he had no choice but to bet his hand.

He went back downstairs and found Clint at the bar, taking another break but not having a beer this time.

"Did he just walk in?" he asked.

"Just a few minutes ago," Clint said.

"What brings him here?"

"He said he came to see me."

"Hmm," Weaver said.

"What?"

"Maybe he heard about the game and came to get into it."

"Did you put out the word?"

"No."

"Then how would he have heard about it?"

"It's kind of a coincidence, him walking in now, don't you think?"

"Not really," Clint said. "After all, you did put out the word that I was dealing for you."

"That's true enough. Well, when he comes down, have Leo bring him on back, huh?"

"Sure, Jed."

"I sure hope this changes things," Weaver said, and walked to the back of the room.

Clint was sure that Short's presence would change the flow of the cards. That happened when you added another hand to a game. He just wasn't all that sure that it was going to change Weaver's luck.

"Is that really Luke Short?" Leo asked from behind Clint.

"That's him."

"I heard he never loses."

"Oh, he loses," Clint said. "Everybody loses sometimes. Luke just doesn't lose very often."

"Clint," Leo said, "the boss is losing a lot of money back there."

Clint turned to look at Leo.

"How much is a lot?"

"A *lot*!" Leo said. "More than I'll ever see. How is letting Luke Short into the game gonna change that, do ya think?"

"It might get better," Clint said, "but then again, it might get worse."

"It can't get much worse," Leo said.

"He's doing that bad?"

"I saw him lose with four jacks—and he was raisin'!"

"With four jacks he'd have to," Clint said. "And he lost?"

Leo nodded.

If that had happened to Clint he would have walked away from the table for a while. There's two schools of thought on that kind of luck. You either ride it out, or walk away from it. When you ride it out you can eventually start taking hands with low pairs, after losing with four of a kind. Sometimes, though, it doesn't change, and you've got to fold them and walk away.

He didn't know if Jed Weaver had ever learned that lesson.

FIFTEEN

At four a.m. that night Clint was having a cup of coffee with Leo, who had just chased the last miner out of the place and locked the doors.

"They're still going at it in the back," Leo said.

"How did it look last time you went back there?"

"Like your friend Luke Short was cleaning up."

"That's no surprise. What about Jed?"

"He didn't look happy."

"Every gambler suffers through a bad streak," Clint commented.

"Not the boss, Mr. Adams," Leo said. "I've never seen him lose."

"How long have you worked for him, Leo?"

"Well, just since he opened this place, but I knew him before then. I just ain't never seen him lose like this."

"Well, luckily he's got the task of building this town to take his mind off of it."

"He thinks about it all the time," Leo said. "He hasn't been paying attention to much else."

"Didn't he just meet with someone about a telegraph line?"

"That meeting didn't go well, either. He lost his temper and walked out."

"How do you know that?"

"Mr. Quinn told me."

"Quinn talks to you?"

"Oh, yeah, a lot," Leo said. "Well, not as much as he used to. See, he and I used to sit like this and talk after we closed."

Great, Clint thought, now Quinn was going to think he was trying to steal his time with Leo.

"Why don't you go back and play?" Leo asked.

"I won't play against him while I'm working for him," Clint explained.

"Then why not go back and watch?"

"I've played in enough big games that I know how they'd react to that," Clint said. "The only people who should be in that room are the players."

"And me, when I deliver drinks."

"Leo, does Jed drink when he plays? I don't remember from the couple of times I played with him."

"Well," Leo said, moving around behind the bar to get a fresh round of drinks for the players, "he didn't in the beginning, but lately he's having me bring him glasses of whiskey. That's not good, is it?"

"Who knows?" Clint said. "Maybe he'll play better when he's drinking. It doesn't work that way for me."

Leo placed all the drinks on a tray and said, "I got to bring these back."

"Let me know how it looks."

As Leo went into the back room Clint poured himself another cup of coffee. He'd wondered, right in the beginning, how well a gambler would do in trying to build a town. How long would it be before the gambling started taking his attention away from what he was trying to do? He hoped this wouldn't happen with Weaver. Up to now the man seemed intent on doing what he had set out to do, build a town that would outlast the gold strike. If he got caught up in trying to ride out a streak of bad luck, he might start paying less attention to Water Hole, and it would suffer. After all, when push came to shove he *was* Water Hole. He had an interest in more than half the businesses in town. If his attention was distracted from his task of building up the town, a lot of people would suffer.

Clint nursed his coffee, anxious to know what was going on in that back room. If he knew Luke Short, he'd made the game his own by now. He'd taken the time to size up the players and knew every nuance and tell of each man's game.

Leo returned, bearing a tray of dirty glasses. He took them behind the bar, then looked at Clint and shook his head. Apparently, Weaver's luck had not taken a turn for the better.

"I'm going to turn in, Leo."

"I couldn't sleep," Leo said. "I'll just wait here and see what happens."

"They could be at it for hours more."

"That's okay," Leo said.

"You're really worried about him, aren't you?"

"He don't look good, Mr. Adams," Leo said, "and the boss is always careful about how he looks."

Clint knew that to be true. Weaver always dressed well, and looked the part of saloon owner, not to mention mayor of the town.

"Well, I'll find out what happened in the morning. Good night, Leo."

"Night, Mr. Adams."

As Leo took some of the dirty glasses into the kitchen, Clint made a detour to the front door. He wanted to find out if he was going to be sleeping alone tonight. If he was, Angela wouldn't be waiting outside for him to let her in.

When he reached the doors he unlocked them and opened one just enough to look outside.

"I thought you'd never open up," Angela said with a smile.

He opened the door wide to let her in. He wasn't sleeping alone tonight.

SIXTEEN

He was up early the next morning, and so was Luke
Short. They had breakfast together and Clint pumped him
about the game.

"Your friend Weaver," Short said, "is having as bad
a run of luck as I've ever seen."

"Bad cards?" Clint asked. "Or bad play?"

"Oh, bad cards, for sure," Short said. "I've never
seen a man lose so many winning hands, if you know
what I mean. Nine times out of ten—ninety-nine times
out of a hundred, even—he would win with the hands
he's been getting."

Leo brought out Short's breakfast, and he raved about
it at first taste.

"By God, man, these are the best flapjacks I've ever
had. What's your secret?"

"That's just it, Mr. Short," Leo said. "It's a secret."

"Well, I won't press you for it," Short said, "I'll just
eat these."

"Luke," Clint said, "what about the others?"

"What about them?"

"Is anyone else losing?"

"Oh, some of the others are losing, but not like Weaver. He's tossing good money after bad—no, that's not

fair. He's had to play the hands he's been dealt. Hell, I'd've been raising like hell with those hands."

"Maybe his luck will change, huh?"

Short shuddered.

"It couldn't get any worse."

The next day Short came down to breakfast again.

"Flapjacks, Mr. Short?" Leo asked.

"You know it, Leo."

Short sat across from Clint.

"If I had a run of luck like Weaver is having," he said, "I'd shoot myself."

"That bad?"

"If it was any worse," he said, "they might as well hoist him up onto the table and take chances at him—if you know what I mean."

Unfortunately, Clint did.

"Somebody should talk to him," Short said.

"About what?"

"About quitting."

"For good?"

"Hell no, just sitting out the rest of this game, and the rest of his bad streak. He's insisting on playing his way out, and it just ain't going to happen."

"Why not?"

"I've seen streaks like this before, Clint," Short said. "This kind of streak breaks people. I mean, it *breaks* their spirit as well as their wallet."

"And how are you doing?"

Short smiled.

"I've made the game my own. It shouldn't be long now."

"Maybe you'll end it tonight."

"Well, for your friend's sake—and mine—let's hope so."

Leo brought his flapjacks out, and Luke Short gave them his undivided attention.

• • •

The third morning Short came down carrying his gear.

"It's over?" Clint asked.

Short nodded and sat at the table. Leo was already on his way with his flapjacks. Short looked down at them fondly and sighed.

"I'm gonna miss these."

"So you're moving on?" Clint asked.

"I cleaned every man jack of them out, Clint," Short said. "Time to find a new game."

"Maybe Weaver will take a break now."

"I don't think so."

"Why not?"

"He's already trying to get up another game," Short said. "He's asked me to stay, and he was badgering some of the others, as well."

"Why doesn't he take a break?"

"He doesn't know how," Short said. "Somebody should have a talk with him, like a friend."

"Oh, some friends should just mind their own business," Clint said.

"Meaning me?" Short asked. "Or you?"

"Both."

"Say no more," Short said. "I'll just concentrate on these cakes."

They finished their breakfast and then Short stood to leave. Clint stood, as well, and shook hands with his friend.

"Thanks a bunch for coming to see me, Luke," Clint said. "We didn't even get a chance to talk."

"Next time," Short said, "whenever or wherever that is."

"Watch yourself, Luke."

"I always do, don't I?" Short asked, and left, after pounding Leo on the back enthusiastically and complimenting him once again on his flapjacks.

SEVENTEEN

No sooner had Short gone out the door than Weaver came stumbling down the stairs. He looked disheveled and needed a bath.

"Did Luke leave?" he asked anxiously.

"You just missed him . . . by half an hour," Clint said. He didn't think it would look good for Weaver to be seen chasing Luke Short down the street.

"Damn it!" he swore.

"Breakfast, boss?" Leo asked.

"Yes, damn it," Weaver said, sitting across from Clint.

"Now that the game's over you can eat, huh?"

"Luke told you about the game?"

"Some."

"He cleaned up."

"He usually does."

"I can beat him."

"So can I, on my best day," Clint said. "These haven't been your best days, have they, Jed?"

"They'll get better," he said.

"Maybe it's time to take some time off."

"A vacation?"

"Not from Water Hole," Clint said, "just from poker."

"Not while I'm running bad."

"Maybe this is the perfect time."

"What do you mean?"

"What have you got to lose by stopping for a while?"

"How will I know when it turns around?"

"The next time you play you'll know."

"And when will that be?"

"I don't know," Clint said. "A week, a month, maybe more."

Weaver stared at him as if he were mad.

"I can't go a month without playing poker."

"Sure you can. You've got this town to build up and keep your mind off of it."

"I'll tell you a secret about this town."

"What?"

"I built it so I'd have people to play cards with," he said, "to gamble with. I wanted miners to come with their gold, and gamblers to come with their wallets, and up until recently it's worked."

"You mean that's why you built the saloon, don't you, Jed?"

Weaver looked across at Clint for a long moment and then said, "Yeah, that's what I meant. What did I say?"

"You said that's why you built the town."

"I did? Ah, I'm tired. It's a good thing *you* knew what I meant."

"Yes," Clint said, "a good thing."

EIGHTEEN

Weaver did have to go a week without playing poker because it took him that long to assemble players for another game. During that week he did concentrate on the business of continuing to build Water Hole and, to Clint, he seemed happier. Clint wished his friend could keep away from the poker table for a month or so, but he doubted it.

Clint's faro luck continued to hold and he was making good money. He was also enjoying himself with Angela, who was not only good in bed, but fun to talk to and be with. All the while he knew that the end of his time in Water Hole was drawing closer and closer.

What he didn't know was that trouble was drawing closer, as well.

Haywood Garr had heard all about Water Hole. He heard that it was a fairly new mining town, but that it was also a rich town. It had a big saloon where a lot of gambling was done, as well as other smaller places, and it also had a bank. Garr was not the kind of man who would get his hands dirty digging gold out of the ground. Not when he could simply take it away from those who did get their hands dirty.

For the job of looting Water Hole he recruited three

men, two of whom he often worked with. Bob Saxon and
Frank Cuddy were his age, midthirties, and the three of
them had pulled many successful jobs together. However,
they had never before looted a whole town. Saxon and
Cuddy were very interested in Garr's plan for doing this.

The fourth man was new to the group. His name was
Chuck Nyfe—the last name pronounced like "knife."
He was in his midtwenties, and seemed to have some
raw talent as a bank robber and all-around thief. Garr had
decided to take the younger man under his wing and de-
velop that talent.

Nyfe was impressed with Garr and listened attentively
to everything the older man had to say. He did not, however, have the same respect for the other two, and was
often arrogant in their presence. For this reason he was
not well liked by them.

The four men were camped a couple of miles outside
of Water Hole, and Garr was explaining his plan.

"We can't just ride in there and take the bank," he
said.

"Why not?" Nyfe asked.

"Because we've got to look it over, Chuck," Garr
said. "See how many lawmen are in town, if the hotel
has guards, see what the security is gonna be like in the
saloon, that sort of thing."

"How long will that take?"

"Days, maybe a week, maybe even more," Garr said.
"We'll just have to be patient."

"What do we do while we're being patient?" Nyfe
asked.

Saxon and Cuddy exchanged a satisfied look. They
knew the answers to all these questions already.

"We wait," Garr said, "and we watch."

"When do we go in?"

"Early tomorrow," Garr said. "We'll camp here the
night and go in when it gets light."

"Together?"

"No," Garr said, liking that the younger man asked that question. It showed that he was thinking. "Bob and Frank will go in first, then you and I later. For the time that we're there no one must know we know each other. Understand?"

"Sure."

"If you see Bob or Frank, just don't speak to them—and the same goes for you guys."

That wasn't a problem for Saxon and Cuddy. They didn't want to talk to Nyfe, anyway.

Saxon and Cuddy were impressed by Water Hole when they first rode in.

"I been to mining towns before," Saxon said. "This one's different."

"How?" his partner asked.

"I'm not sure," Saxon said, "it just feels . . . different."

"Is it bigger?"

"Some, maybe, but that ain't all of it."

Cuddy didn't know what Saxon was talking about, so he didn't bother thinking about it.

They left their horses at the livery and went in search of a room.

A couple of hours later Garr rode in with Nyfe. When they passed the bank, Nyfe craned his neck for a look.

"Face front, damn it," Garr said.

"You said we had to check out the bank."

"Yeah, but you don't have to be so obvious about it."

"So how do we do it?"

"We go in and open an account."

"We put money *in* the bank?"

"Just a little bit," Garr said. "That way we get a good look at the inside."

"That's smart."

"I know."

"And there's the gambling house," Nyfe said. " 'The Crystal Palace,' " he read, as they went by. "Looks pretty big."

"We'll go in and take a look at that, too."

"I'll bet a place like this has a real good cathouse, too," Nyfe said. "We gonna take a look at that?"

"You can, if you want," Garr said. "I don't take up with diseased whores."

"Who says they're diseased?"

"They're whores, aren't they?" Garr asked.

Nyfe liked Garr and thought he could learn a lot from him, but he didn't understand this attitude toward whores. He *loved* women, and whores were women, and that's all he cared about.

"Where are we gonna stay?" he asked.

"We'll leave the horses at the livery and then take a look around town," Garr said. "Maybe we can find a rooming house."

"Why not just go to the hotel?"

"Because we don't want to be noticed, that's why."

Maybe, Garr thought, tired of fielding Nyfe's questions, the younger man didn't have all that much potential, after all.

NINETEEN

Although Ollie Quinn was technically the sheriff of Water Hole, there was no sheriff's office, and there was no jail. Haywood Garr noticed this immediately.

"So there's no law," Nyfe said. "That's good."

"There's no jail," Garr said, "that don't mean there's no law. Don't jump to conclusions."

"But what if—"

"Do me a favor for now, Chuck?"

"What's that?"

"Stop asking questions."

Ollie Quinn entered Jed Weaver's office and found his boss and friend behind his desk, smoking a cigar.

"You look happy," Quinn said.

"Why shouldn't I be?"

"Well, except for the fact that you've had a run of bad luck, I can't think why. Everything's going great as far as the town is concerned."

"You're right about that."

"Except for the telegraph wire."

"I'm still working on that from another angle," Weaver said.

"So that's why you look happy?"

"No," Weaver said, inspecting the glowing tip of his cigar, "I've got a game together."

"Ah."

"Clint was right," Weaver went on, "taking a week off from poker was the right thing to do. My negative frame of mind is gone. I'm going to approach this game with a fresh outlook."

"When does it start?"

"Two days," Weaver said. "Players should start arriving today."

"Anybody I should know about, as sheriff?"

"I don't think so," Weaver said. "These are gamblers, not gunmen or troublemakers."

"Like Adams?"

Weaver pointed his cigar at Quinn.

"You have to admit you were wrong about that."

"I do?"

"There hasn't been any trouble around him, has there?" Weaver asked. "Admit it."

"I admit," Quinn said, "that he hasn't brought us any trouble . . . yet."

"You're pessimistic, Quinn," Weaver said. "You need a fresh outlook, like mine."

"My outlook is just fine, thanks," Quinn said. "I'm going to take a turn around the town."

"You take your job as sheriff seriously, don't you?" Weaver asked.

"No less seriously than you take your job as mayor."

As Quinn went out the door Weaver called out, "There's no need to be sarcastic!"

Once in a while Clint skipped breakfast with Leo and went to a café down the street. This was one of those days, and he was going out the door as Quinn was.

The two men simply nodded to each other as they went out. There hadn't been much conversation between them over the past week.

"It looks like you got your way," Quinn said when they were outside, surprising Clint.

"How's that?"

"Jed took a week off from poker," Quinn said. "That's what you wanted him to do, wasn't it?"

"I just thought he should give his luck a chance to change on its own."

"Well, maybe it worked," Quinn said. "He's got another game set up in two days. Players should start arriving today."

"Why are you telling me this?"

"Because," Quinn said, "you know these people better than I do. I want you to tell me if somebody comes to town that I should be worried about."

"Worried in what way?"

"That he might bring trouble with him."

"The way I did?"

"The way you still might."

"You know," Clint said, "we were doing much better when we weren't talking to each other."

"That suits me," Quinn said, and turned and walked away—which puzzled Clint. After all, hadn't he started the conversation in the first place?

Ollie Quinn continued to baffle Clint, and he decided the only way to handle the man was to ignore him.

Clint didn't like the way things had started going lately in Water Hole. He had accepted Weaver's offer to come here in order to be on the ground floor of something new, something with the potential to be big. Instead Weaver was fighting his bad luck to the detriment of everything else, and Clint was not getting along at all with Ollie Quinn, Weaver's right-hand man. He was getting closer and closer to pulling up stakes and going back out on the trail, where he belonged.

He decided to take a ride. It would clear his head and give Duke some exercise. In the livery the big black stared at him, almost accusingly, as he saddled him, craning his massive neck to look back at him.

"I know," Clint said to his old friend, "you don't like it when we're in one place for too long."

Duke looked away.

"Let's just go out and stretch our legs, old boy," Clint said, patting Duke's neck. He led the big black outside and then mounted up.

Riding out of town he spotted two men going into a boardinghouse and frowned. He thought he recognized one of them. If he was right, then there was a potential for trouble in town—but averting trouble was Sheriff Quinn's job. Let him worry about it. Besides, maybe he hadn't seen who he thought he had.

When he and Duke cleared town Clint allowed Duke to break into a run and left his Water Hole problems behind.

Haywood Garr couldn't believe his eyes when he saw the man riding on the big black. He didn't say anything to Nyfe, but he was pretty sure the man was Clint Adams. He wouldn't mention it to the others, either. Not until he was sure.

TWENTY

Garr managed to get a room at the front of the boarding-house so he could see out the window. Chuck Nyfe wanted to go out and see the town, and Garr told him to go ahead. He told him not to be obvious but to remember everything he saw.

Once Nyfe was gone Garr heaved a sigh of relief. It was good to be away from the constant questions. After this job he would never take another kid "under his wing." He was only going to work with seasoned professionals he knew.

Aside from wanting to get away from Nyfe's incessant chatter, Garr wanted to sit by the front window and wait for the man on the black horse to come back. He wanted to be *sure* that the man he had seen was the Gunsmith. If he was, then Garr was going to have to determine what his place was in the town of Water Hole. If he was just passing through, then they could wait for him to leave. If he was staying, they had to know where, and what he was doing.

And then there was the other problem. Clint Adams knew him. If Adams saw him, what would he do? After all, the man knew what Haywood Garr did for a living, but Adams was no lawman.

What would he do?

• • •

Clint rode back into town the way he came, and gave the boardinghouse a sideways glance as he went by. He did not know that he was giving Garr the opportunity to positively identify him.

He took Duke back to the livery and thought about the man he thought he *might* have seen. Haywood Garr was a thief. He robbed banks, stagecoaches, trains, and anything else you could think of, and he managed to stay one step ahead of the law, and the bounty hunters. If he was in Water Hole it meant he was looking for a score—and there were plenty of them to be had here. He could go after the bank, the Crystal Palace, even the private game, if he knew about it. There was always a lot of money on the table in a private game.

He decided to wait until he was sure. If that happened, if Garr was actually in town, then he wouldn't go to Quinn, but to Weaver. Then if Jed Weaver wanted to relay that information to Ollie Quinn, that was his business. Clint would simply make sure that his friend knew that a known thief was in town, and let him take it from there.

After all, it was Jed Weaver's town.

TWENTY-ONE

Clint decided there were two ways of finding out if the man he saw was Haywood Garr. One would be to go to the boardinghouse, knock on the door, and ask. The second would be to sit out in front of the Crystal Palace in a wooden chair and wait to see if Garr walked by. Clint believed that in a western town if you simply sat in one place long enough everyone would walk past you.

He decided to test out his belief.

At breakfast with Weaver they talked about his new game.

"This is just what I need to turn it all around, Clint," Weaver said enthusiastically.

"You don't think you're rushing into another game too soon, Jed?"

"Not at all," Weaver said. "I've got five new players lined up—six, if you'll play."

"I haven't changed my mind about that," Clint said. "I won't play against you while I'm working for you."

"What if I fired you?"

"It wouldn't make a difference."

"I'm just kidding."

"I know you are."

Weaver pushed his chair back and stood up.

83

"A couple of the players arrived yesterday, and the other three should be here today. What are you going to do with your day?"

"I just thought I'd take it easy, sit outside and watch the town go by for a while."

"Well, if anyone arrives looking for me I'll be in the office."

"I'll tell them."

Weaver went into his office and Clint stood up, preparing to leave. Before he could, though, Leo came out of the kitchen and stopped him.

"Do you think it's a good idea for the boss to play in another game so soon?"

"No, I don't," Clint said, "but I can't tell him that, Leo."

"Why not?"

"Because he wouldn't listen to me, that's why. He's going to have to figure it out for himself."

"What if he starts winning?"

"Well," Clint said, "that would be good and bad. Good for him to stop losing, but bad because I don't think he'd have learned anything from his first losing streak."

"What should he be learning?"

"That you can't win all the time, Leo," Clint said. "It just doesn't happen. Didn't you learn that when you stopped fighting?"

"No," Leo said, "I never lost a fight, Clint."

Clint stared at the big man.

"You *never* lost a fight?" he repeated.

"That's right."

"Well, then, take my word for it, Leo," Clint said. "If you had continued to fight you would have lost one day."

"If you say so."

"I'll be sitting out front if anyone's looking for me."

Clint went outside, pulled over a chair, and sat down. He couldn't believe that Leo had never lost a fight. He would have to ask the man later just how many fights he had had—but the fact that he'd never lost made him a perfect employee for Weaver who, up until recently, had never had a bad losing streak.

It had been Clint's experience that losing streaks went on for a long time—not just days or weeks, but sometimes months, or even years. Somehow, he doubted that changing the game and the players was the answer for Weaver. The man had to learn something from this, or the experience would be wasted.

Maybe Luke Short had been right. Maybe a friend should talk to Weaver about it.

Clint just didn't necessarily want to be that friend.

TWENTY-TWO

In one respect Clint's theory seemed to be working out. He'd been sitting in front of the Palace for half a day and already he had seen several people two and three times, on their way to or from some kind of work or errand, apparently.

He also discovered that the people in Water Hole were fairly friendly. They greeted him when they went by, and they weren't all people who knew him from the saloon. In fact, most of the people who passed he was sure he'd never seen at his faro table, or even in the Palace. There were certainly more people in the town of Water Hole than went into the Crystal Palace in the evenings.

From Clint's vantage point he was able to look down the block and see the bank. He wasn't sure his plan for spotting Haywood Garr was going to work until he finally saw the man go into the bank. He got out of his chair quickly and walked down the block until he was standing across from the bank. If Garr was going to try anything, he was going to find Clint waiting for him when he came out.

Garr saw Clint Adams sitting in front of the saloon. Okay, so Adams had positively identified him, so what?

He wasn't doing anything wrong. All he was doing was going into the bank and opening an account. Nobody could say anything about that.

He opened the account with one of the tellers, depositing twenty dollars.

"It's not much," he said to the young woman.

"Every dollar helps," she said cheerfully. "You just come in every week and put some money in and you'll see how it grows."

"I will, won't I?" he asked, smiling. "Thank you."

With that he turned and walked out of the bank, and saw Clint Adams standing across the street. He thought, what the hell, why wait? He started across toward the Gunsmith.

Clint was about to start across the street when he saw Garr save him the trouble. The man stepped off the boardwalk and crossed the street.

"What are you doing here, Garr?" he asked as the man reached him.

"What, no hello for an old friend?" Garr asked.

"We're not friends, Garr," Clint said. "I've got better taste in friends."

"Acquaintances, then," Garr said. "You can't argue with that word."

"Oh, we're acquainted, all right," Clint said. "Well enough to know that you weren't in that bank just to open an account."

"Actually, I was," Garr said, and showed Clint his receipt.

"I thought I recognized you earlier today," Clint said. "I know where you're staying."

Garr shrugged and said, "So what? I haven't done anything."

"Not here," Clint said, "not yet."

"Come on, Adams," Garr said. "There's plenty of room in this gold town for both of us."

"I don't know what game you're playing, Garr," Clint said, "but you can bet I'll be watching you."

"Why? You ain't the sheriff of this town, are you?"

"Hardly."

"Then what's it to you?"

"I like this town," Clint said. "I've been here for months and it's quiet, for the most part. I want to keep it that way."

"Hey," Garr said, spreading his hands, "I like a quiet town as much as the next guy. Maybe I'll like this one enough to settle down. What do you think of that?"

"Do yourself a favor, Garr."

"What's that?"

"Find another place."

"If I didn't know you better I'd think that was a threat. Is there a lawman in this town I can report that to?"

"You don't know me at all, Garr," Clint said, "and trust me, you don't want to meet the sheriff here."

"So there is one?"

"You bet there is one."

"Well, that's good," Garr said. "I feel safer just knowing that."

"What do you want here, Garr?"

"Me? I'm just passing through."

"So if you're just passing through why did you open a bank account?"

Clint thought he had the man there, but Garr answered smoothly, without getting ruffled.

"I like to know my money's safe—but I did notice something odd about that bank."

"What's that?"

"It doesn't have a safe," Garr said. "Don't you find that strange?"

"They don't need a safe. They've got plenty of security."

"Well, I'm glad I stopped to talk to you, then. You've

just made me feel better about my safety, and the safety of my money.''

"Remember what I said, Garr,'' Clint said. "Find someplace else to feel safe.''

Garr smiled and started to walk away.

"And if you've got any friends in town with you, tell them the same thing.''

"What makes you think I have friends in town?''

"Because men like you travel in packs, Garr,'' Clint said. "You don't feel safe traveling alone.''

"Do I look like I'm worried about being alone?'' Garr asked, spreading his arms.

"I know you, Garr,'' Clint said, "maybe like you think you know me.''

"You gonna be in town long, Adams?''

"Long enough to make sure you don't pull anything.''

"You're gonna be wasting your time watching me, Adams,'' Garr said.

"It's my time to waste, isn't it?''

Garr waved a hand, turned, and walked away.

Haywood Garr hated when he felt challenged, and he felt challenged now. He knew that he should get the boys and move on to another town, but the Gunsmith was a challenge all by himself. Throw in this gold-rich town, and it was too much for him to pass up. The only question in his mind was how much to tell the others. What would they say and do if they knew they might have to face the Gunsmith?

Clint watched Haywood Garr walk away. He *knew* the man wouldn't have come to town alone. For one thing he had already seen him with one other man. If he was here to pull some kind of a job, he probably had at least three men with him. That meant two other men had ridden into town, either before Garr or after him. They wouldn't have come in together because they wouldn't want to attract attention that way.

Ollie Quinn had asked Clint to let him know if he saw someone who might be trouble. Well, with a man like Garr there was no ''might'' involved. He was trouble as sure as the sun was shining every day. The only question was should he tell Quinn or Weaver. But Garr wasn't really a danger to Weaver and his Crystal Palace. It was more likely he and his men were there for the bank, since he'd taken a look inside of it.

In any other town Clint would have gone right to the sheriff. In Water Hole he had to think twice about it, but in the end he decided that was what he had to do.

TWENTY-THREE

Clint went inside the Crystal Palace, which was doing a brisk afternoon business. Leo was still behind the bar.

"Leo, have you seen Quinn today?"

"I seen him."

"Where?"

"Here."

"Is he still here?"

"I doubt it."

"Where is he, then?"

"I don't know . . . but I could guess."

The way Leo said it, Clint could guess, too.

The Water Hole Social Club.

When Clint entered he saw Angela sitting in the living room with the other girls. The club did not do a brisk business when it was still light out. It was hard for husbands to sneak into the place when the sun was shining. Still, the girls always had to make themselves available.

When she saw him she bounced up off the sofa and trotted over to him.

"What are you doing here?"

"I'm looking for Quinn."

"Oh."

He waited a moment, then asked, "Is he here?"

"We're not supposed to say."

"So he is here, and he's with Danielle."

"He don't pay her," Angela said. "She's not one of the girls, but they're . . . kinda involved."

"I need to talk to him, Angela."

Her eyes went wide.

"We're not supposed to bother him when he's, you know, here."

"Somebody has to go up and tell him I'm here," Clint said.

"I can't," she said, "and the others won't."

"Well," he said, "I'll have to do it myself, then," and he started for the stairs.

Angela moved quickly, getting between him and the stairs.

"You ain't allowed upstairs without a girl, Clint."

"Well," he said, "you're a girl. Take me up and show me Danielle's room."

"I could get in trouble."

"Believe me, Angela," Clint said, "you'll get in more trouble if you don't."

"Honest?"

"Honest."

"A-all right. I'll show you which room it is, but you knock on the door."

"Deal."

"Come on, then."

She led the way and he followed.

Inside Danielle's room Ollie Quinn was very involved with Danielle. He was straddling her and his penis was buried deep inside of her. She was moaning and hanging on to him as he pounded into her, harder and harder, until both of them were coming very near . . .

. . . and there was a knock on the door.

Quinn yelled out loud, almost a roar, and Danielle

shouted, "What is it?" her voice quavering.

"*Who* is it, damn it?" Quinn shouted.

"It's Clint Adams."

"What?"

"What does he want?" she asked, looking up at him.

"Go away, Adams!"

"I've got to talk to you, Quinn. It's urgent."

"No no no no," Danielle said, "not now, I'm so *close*!"

"Later, Adams—"

"I'll wait downstairs, Quinn," Clint called back. "You finish what you're doing and I'll wait downstairs."

They heard Clint's footsteps retreat.

"What should we do?" Danielle asked.

"You heard the man," Quinn growled. "We'll finish what we're doing."

Quinn came downstairs twenty minutes later like he owned the place. He was wearing only his trousers, his feet and torso bare. Clint heard some of the girls catch their breath because there was no doubt that he was a handsome man, and well built.

"This better be damned good!" he snapped at Clint.

"You asked me to tell you if I saw somebody in town who might be trouble."

"And?"

"There's no might about it," Clint said. "I saw Haywood Garr in town and spoke to him."

Quinn frowned.

"Why do I know that name?"

"Because," Clint said slowly, "he robs banks."

"Oh, *that* Haywood Garr."

"Yes, that one."

"And he's here?"

"Yes."

"You saw him?"

"And spoke to him."

"And I suppose he admitted he was here to rob the bank?" Quinn asked.

"No," Clint said, "but he did go into the bank and make a deposit."

"Lots of people make deposits in the bank," Quinn said. "It doesn't mean they're going to rob it."

"Other people are not Haywood Garr, Quinn."

Quinn thought a moment, then asked, "Is he alone?"

"I doubt it," Clint said. "He was when I talked to him, but I spotted him earlier and he was with one other man. If he's going to pull a job he'll have at least two more somewhere around town."

"You seem to know him pretty well."

"Well enough."

"Where's he staying?"

"In a boardinghouse at the north end of town."

"I'll get dressed and we'll go and talk to him." He turned to go to the stairs.

"We? What do you mean, we?" Clint asked.

Quinn turned back.

"You're not gonna back me up?"

"Do you want me to back you up?"

Quinn stared at Clint and then said, "Oh, I see. You want me to ask you."

"It would be nice," Clint said. "After all, you've made it real clear that you don't want me in Water Hole. Why should I volunteer to help you?"

Quinn glared at him for a few moments, turning the situation over in his head. He could handle Haywood Garr, even if he had another man with him. However, if he had *three* men with him—or more—he could end up getting killed. He hated asking Clint Adams for help, but he'd hate getting killed even more.

"All right, then."

"All right, what?"

"I'll ask you."

Clint folded his arms.

"Go ahead . . . ask."

Quinn gritted his teeth.

"Will you help me brace Garr and his men?"

"What do you want to do?"

"Talk to them," Quinn said, "let them know we're onto them, and warn them out of town."

"They won't go."

"That's how I want to play it . . . first," Quinn said.

"All right, Quinn," Clint said, after a moment. "You're the sheriff. We'll play it your way."

"I'll get dressed," Quinn said, "and get my gun."

"I'll be waiting right here."

TWENTY-FOUR

Clint and Quinn walked down to the boardinghouse together and Quinn knocked on the door.

"This place is run by Artie Dolan and his wife. They staked a claim, but it was one of the ones that petered out real quick. But they made enough money to open this place."

The door was opened by a red-faced man in his thirties.

"Quinn. What can I do for you?"

"I'm here as sheriff, Artie," Quinn said. "You got some strangers staying here?"

"Two," Dolan said. "They got here today. Why? They troublemakers?"

"Could be. Are they in now?"

"No, they went out. When they come back should I not let them in, Sheriff?"

"Don't do anything unusual," Quinn said. "They haven't done anything yet. I'm just checking on them."

After a few more moments of soothing Dolan and convincing him that he didn't have to do anything, Quinn and Clint left.

"We'll have to look around town for them," Quinn said. "Maybe they're checking out the bank again."

"I'll go once around the town with you, Quinn, and then I'm done. This is your job, anyway. Don't you have any deputies?"

"No."

"Maybe you'd better get some."

"What about you?"

"Oh, no," Clint said. "I don't mind helping out, some, but I'm not wearing a badge."

"You did once."

"A long time ago," Clint said. "It's more trouble than it's worth."

"All right, then," Quinn said, firming his jaw, "once around the town."

They found Garr and another man—Chuck Nyfe—in one of the smaller saloons. They stopped to look inside and Clint spotted them at a table.

"There," he said.

"Where?"

"Center of the room. Dark-haired fella with a younger man."

"I see 'em."

They stepped into the saloon. Garr noticed Clint right away.

"Brought a friend this time, Adams?" he asked.

"Garr, this is Sheriff Quinn," Clint said. "He wants a word with you."

"What can I do for you, Sheriff?"

"You can get out of town," Quinn said, "you and your young friend."

"We ain't done nothin'," Nyfe said belligerently.

"I'm not talking to you, boy," Quinn said.

Nyfe's face turned red and he started to get up. Quinn reached out, clamped a hand on the man's shoulder and pushed him back down in his chair. Nyfe tried to rise again, but Quinn squeezed and suddenly Nyfe was cringing in pain.

"Just sit tight," Quinn said, and released his hold. Nyfe couldn't help reaching up himself and rubbing his shoulder.

"Why are you orderin' us out of town, Sheriff?" Garr asked. "We ain't done nothing. This ain't right."

"It doesn't matter whether you've done something or not," Quinn said. "I want you out of town. It's that simple."

"You can't do that."

"Sure I can," Quinn said. "I'm the sheriff, remember?"

"But . . . it ain't legal!" Nyfe said, still holding his shoulder.

"Boy," Quinn said, "you speak again if I haven't spoken to you and you're gonna hurt a lot worse."

Nyfe wanted to say something back but he didn't dare.

"Now, Mr. Garr, you and your friend—and any other friends you might have in town—mount up and ride out by morning. If I see you in town tomorrow you're gonna be sorry."

"What are you gonna do, kill me?" Garr asked.

"Well, now, that would make you dead, not sorry," Quinn said.

"Sorry's worse than dead?" Nyfe asked. He couldn't help himself.

Quinn grinned, and it wasn't pretty.

"It is when it's me making you sorry."

"Forget it, kid," Garr said. "He's just tryin' to scare you."

"Not at all," Quinn said. "I'm just stating a fact. You would both do well to remember what I said."

"And what do you have to say, Adams?" Garr asked.

"Nothing," Clint said. "He's the law, he does all the talking."

"So what are you doing here?"

"I'm pointing you out to him," Clint said, "and making sure he doesn't get shot in the back."

Garr stiffened.

"I don't shoot people in the back!"

"Then that's about the only place you draw the line, isn't it, Garr?"

"Just remember what I said, Garr," Quinn said. "Gone by morning."

With that Quinn turned and walked out. Clint backed out, not taking Garr at his word about back-shooting.

Outside Quinn said, "Well, that takes care of that. I guess I won't be needing you anymore."

"That's it?" Clint asked. "You think he's just going to leave in the morning?"

"Why wouldn't he?"

"Because you didn't scare him, Quinn," Clint said. "You scared the younger one, but you didn't scare Garr."

"But he knows I know him now," Quinn argued. "He wouldn't dare try anything."

"This is just the time he would try something," Clint said. "He knows you think he won't."

Quinn thought a moment, then said, "He's a common thief. Is he capable of that kind of thinking?"

"He's cunning, Quinn," Clint said. "In his business that's better than being smart, intelligent, or uncommon."

Quinn paused to think again and digest what Clint had said. Clint had to give the man credit. He did listen.

"What do you suggest, then?"

"That you have someone watch him and see if he contacts his other men."

"You're sure there are others?"

"If he came here to pull a job, there are others," Clint said. "And if he didn't, then you don't have a problem."

"I could watch him myself."

"He'd spot you in a minute," Clint said. "You need

someone who can blend in with the background. Do you know anyone like that in town?''

"I might," Quinn said. "I'll have to think about it."

"Well, think quick," Clint said. "Don't give him a chance to contact the others without you knowing about it. And I'd double the guard on the bank tonight, and for as long as Garr is here."

"He won't be here long," Quinn said. "I meant what I said. If he's still here in the morning he's going to be sorry."

"Well, you let me know when you intend to make him sorry," Clint said, "and I'll back you up again. I don't want your death on my conscience."

"You don't think I can take a man like Garr?"

"I don't think the men he has with him will be as squeamish as he is about back-shooting you."

Quinn frowned and said, "You have a point. All right, I'll come and get you before I do anything."

"Good. I'm going to go and do what Weaver pays me for now. I'll see you later."

"All right."

Clint started walking toward the Crystal Palace, then turned back.

"Quinn."

"Yes?"

"Watch your back."

"I will," he said, then after a pause he added, "thanks."

TWENTY-FIVE

Clint was not surprised when he saw Haywood Garr in the Crystal Palace that night. If he'd kept his ears open during the day he would have found out that Quinn also worked at the Palace. Garr was the kind of man who scouted every aspect of a job, and that included the local lawman.

He was alone when he came in, and another man slipped in after him. Clint didn't know him, but he figured this was the man Quinn had put on Garr to keep an eye on him. He was a small man, dressed like a miner, and he blended into the background just fine. Quinn had made a good choice.

Garr took up a position at the bar, ordered a beer, and nursed it. Quinn wasn't in the room, but he had put an extra man in the saloon just in case, so that there was now a man on the platform with a shotgun, and one on the floor. Garr took notice of both of them.

When Clint took a break he walked to the bar and got a beer from Leo. Garr, several feet further down the bar, closed the gap and stood next to Clint.

"Had to give me up to the law, didn't you?"

"I'm not the law, Garr," Clint said. "There was nothing else I could do."

105

"Where is your friend the sheriff? I heard he works here, as well."

"He's in charge of security here, among other things," Clint said.

"Yeah, I saw the two men with shotguns. Does he think that would stop anyone who really wanted to take this place?"

"You don't want this place, Garr," Clint said. "You want the bank."

"How do you know what I want?"

Clint looked at him for the first time.

"Because I've known men like you all my life. You want what you can't have, and the more somebody tells you you can't have it, the more you want it."

"Is that so?"

"Yes," Clint said, "that's so."

There was a moment of silence between them which Clint broke.

"Where's your young friend? Too scared to come out on the street?"

"I made him stay at the boardinghouse. I didn't want him getting me killed."

"Where'd you pick him up, anyway?"

"I thought he had some talent, some potential."

"None of that is any good without nerve," Clint said. "Quinn had him peeing himself."

"I know," Garr said with a sour look.

"Good thing you've got some of your good men along with you, huh?"

Garr smiled.

"Nice try, Adams. When did you start dealing faro? That's not something I heard you did."

"I'm new at it," Clint said, "but I've got some talent and potential." He put his empty beer mug down.

"And nerve?"

"Come and find out."

"No," Garr said, shaking his head. "I know better than to play another man's game."

"If you do," Clint said, "then you're a lot smarter than I gave you credit for."

"Well," Garr said, "I think I'll take that as a compliment."

"Don't," Clint said. "I'm not in the habit of handing out compliments to scum."

He felt Garr stiffen and then turned and walked to the faro table, testing Garr's remark about not shooting people in the back.

The small of his back itched like mad all the way to the table.

TWENTY-SIX

When Quinn finally appeared in the Crystal Palace, Garr was still standing at the bar. Clint could see that Quinn noticed him, but although Garr had been warned out of town by morning, he had not been warned away from the Palace.

Quinn came over to Clint's table while there was a lull and he had no players.

"How long has he been here?" he asked.

"About an hour."

"He's got nerve."

"You didn't tell him not to come here."

"You've got a point."

"His tail followed him in," Clint said. "You seem to have made the right choice, there."

"I'll find out for sure later."

"What's your man's name?"

"His name's Max. He does odd jobs in town."

"Well, he blends in well enough. Let's just hope he's not spotted."

"He can take care of himself."

"Not against a man like Garr."

Quinn didn't reply.

"Any word on Jed's game?"

"It starts the day after tomorrow," Quinn said. "All of the players have arrived in town."

"Do you know any of them?"

"No," Quinn said. "Maybe you do." He named them, five gamblers, three of whom Clint had heard of but never met.

"Are they any good?"

"They're not Luke Short," Clint said, "but they make a living at it."

"If he starts losing again . . ." Quinn said, then stopped.

"What?" Clint asked. "What are you afraid will happen, Quinn?"

For the first time since Clint had met him, Quinn looked unsure of himself.

"I don't know," Quinn said. "I just have a bad feeling." He looked around. "Where is everybody?"

"I've been wondering that myself," Clint said. "It's been a slow night. In fact, it's been a slow week."

"Maybe the miners have finally decided to keep the gold for themselves."

"That would not be good news for Jed."

"Maybe not," Quinn said, "but not as bad news as if the mines had started to dry up."

"Is that what you're thinking?" Clint asked. "That the strike is petering out?"

Quinn didn't answer.

"Do you think Water Hole is in a position to survive that yet?"

Now Quinn shook his head.

"It's too soon," he said. "If it's happening, it's too damn soon."

"What have you heard?" Clint asked. "Have you heard some talk?"

"No," Quinn said, "no talk, it's just . . . things have slowed down. It's not only slow here, but at the social club, as well."

"Have you talked to Jed about your feelings?"

"No," Quinn said. "I don't think he'd listen. He's too intent on this next game."

"But if it's happening he should be made aware of it," Clint said.

"I don't know that it is happening," Quinn replied. "When I do know, I'll say something."

With that Quinn walked away. He walked to each of his men and spoke to them in turn, probably telling them to watch Garr.

However, when Clint looked over at the bar Haywood Garr was gone. He didn't see him anywhere. He hadn't seen him walk out, but then he'd been talking to Quinn. He looked around for the man who was tailing Garr, but he was gone, too. Clint looked at Quinn and saw that he, too, was aware that Garr was suddenly gone.

But gone where?

TWENTY-SEVEN

They found Max's body the next morning, and came for Quinn. Clint didn't hear about it until breakfast, when Leo told him.

"How was he killed?"

"Knife," Leo said. "Somebody cut his throat."

"Where's Quinn?"

"He left earlier, when they came and got him."

If Quinn had gone after Garr alone . . .

"Hey," Leo shouted as Clint headed for the door, "you didn't finish your breakfast!"

Clint found Quinn at the undertaker's, arranging for Max's burial.

"What was his last name?" the undertaker was asking as Clint entered.

"I don't know," Quinn said. "He was only known as Max."

"Maybe that was his last name?"

"Just put Max on his grave," Quinn said testily. He turned as Clint approached. "I know what you're going to say."

"What?"

"That I got him killed," Quinn said. "That I should

have gotten someone better suited—but you said I needed to do it quickly.''

"I'm not blaming you, Quinn," Clint said. "Did you get to talk to him last night?"

"No," Quinn said, "we were supposed to meet this morning."

"Where was he found?"

"In an alley next to the feed and grain."

"You're thinking it was Garr?"

"Who else?"

Clint shrugged.

"Is he known to use a knife?" Quinn asked.

"No."

"Maybe he has someone with him who is."

"Have you checked the boardinghouse for him?"

"Not yet."

"I'll go with you."

"Fine," Quinn said, "let's go."

They left the undertaker's together and walked to the house. When Artie Dolan answered the door he said, "They're gone."

"Why didn't you come and get me?" Quinn asked.

"I didn't know I was supposed to," the man said. "They got up early, paid me, and left. I didn't know."

"Never mind," Quinn said. "Forget it."

Dolan closed the door and Quinn turned to Clint.

"Why would they kill him if they were going to leave town?" he asked.

"They wouldn't," Clint said, "but they'd kill him to keep him from telling you what he saw."

"The other two men."

"Right."

"So where are they now?"

"Who knows?"

"But you don't think they've gone."

"I doubt it."

"Then they'll try for the bank."

"That's my guess."

"Then that's where I'll be," Quinn said, "waiting for them."

TWENTY-EIGHT

Quinn remained inside the bank all day, with two guards armed with shotguns. Later in the day he even pulled one of his men out of the saloon. That left only one man on the platform in the Crystal Palace that evening. Clint was at his faro table. Quinn had told him he didn't need him at the bank. He had enough help with the security guards. Clint decided to let Quinn play it his own way.

The next morning, at breakfast, Quinn asked for advice.

"Nothing happened yesterday."

"I know."

"Should we stand guard again today?"

"I don't know, Quinn." Clint was annoyed that Quinn, after ignoring him for so long, was now constantly asking for help. He liked it better when the man was ignoring him. Of course, it was probably his fault for having offered his help in the first place.

"I need you to guess, Adams," Quinn said. "You know this man's mind better than I do."

"He's going to do one of three things," Clint said finally.

"And what are they?"

"One, he's going to hit the bank, but make you wait.

In fact, he might wait long enough for you to give up on him.''

''And two?''

''He's going to hit the Palace.''

''The Palace? Why?''

''He must have heard about the big game by now,'' Clint said. ''While he's got your attention on the bank, he'll hit the game.''

''And three?''

''He's gone.''

''I like that last one,'' Quinn said. ''I can't watch the bank and the game.''

''You'll have to pick one,'' Clint said.

''But which one?'' Quinn asked. ''And once I choose, what happens to the other one?''

''I don't know, Quinn.''

Quinn thought a moment while Clint continued to eat his breakfast. The other man was only having coffee.

''I've got to stay with the bank,'' Quinn said finally. ''That's where I think he'll hit.''

''Fine.''

''But then there's the game.''

''Put some men on both.''

''I can't,'' Quinn said. ''I've got two bank guards and two men working the saloon. If there are four robbers I'll need all the men I can get.''

''You left one man here last night.''

''But you were here, too,'' Quinn said. ''I knew if anything happened you could handle it, you and the guard, and Jed.''

''What are you saying?''

''I need you to close your table tonight and watch the game.''

''If I close my table I don't make any money.''

''Clint, I need your help. If they hit the game somebody could get killed. If it's *Jed*, then none of us are going to make any money anymore.''

"You make a convincing argument. All right. Keep your man on the platform, and I'll stay in the room with the game."

"Good. I'll clear it with Jed."

"Will he go along with it?"

"Yes."

"No," Jed Weaver said.

"Why not?" Quinn demanded.

"Because none of the other players will want a man in the room if he's not playing."

"But if the game gets robbed—"

"Everyone in that room has a gun."

"How many of them have a gambler's hide-out gun up their sleeve?" Quinn asked. "What good is a two-shot derringer gonna do against four armed robbers?"

"Then put your guards outside the door."

"I want a man inside."

"Why?"

"What if one of the poker players is in on it?"

That stopped Weaver cold.

"You don't know all of them personally, do you?" Quinn asked. "What if one of them is not who he says he is?"

"This is the first day of the game," Weaver said. "I don't want them spooked."

"Why not? Maybe they won't play as well if they are spooked."

"I want them to play well," Weaver said. "How will I know if my streak is over if they don't?"

"Then what do you suggest?"

Weaver thought a moment and then said, "I have an idea." He told it to Quinn.

"Will Adams go along with it?"

"I think so."

•   •   •

"No," Clint said.

"Why not?" Quinn demanded.

"I've told Jed I won't play against him while I work for him."

"Then quit," Quinn said, "just long enough to do this."

"No."

"Your table's gonna be closed, anyway."

"No."

"You could win a lot of money."

"No."

"Damn it, Clint," Quinn said, "it's the only way—if you say no again I'll kick your ass all the way out the door!"

Clint stared at Quinn just long enough for the man to get antsy.

"You make a convincing argument."

He was going to do it, anyway.

TWENTY-NINE

So there were seven players when the game started, not six. As far as any of the others knew, Clint was simply another player. Jed Weaver was the only one who knew he was there more as a guard. However, he made sure that Clint promised to play his best.

"I'd better play my best," Clint said, "I'm using your money."

This had been a condition of Clint's playing, that Weaver—who wanted him in the game—would put up his stake.

"I'll be playing against my own money," Weaver complained.

"I'm not really supposed to be there as a player, am I?" Clint asked. "What does it matter whose money I'm using?"

"I'll be winning my own money."

"And if I lose, I'll be losing your money. And if the game is robbed, all of the money would disappear."

"Do you really think one of the players is in on this?" Weaver asked. They were sitting in his office, across the desk from each other, with the game scheduled to start in half an hour.

"I know the names of three of the men you're playing,'' Clint said. ''Hal Cornwall, Ken Block, and Brett Ells. They're all professional gamblers I've heard of, but I've never seen any of them. The other two men are unknown to both of us, right?''

''Right.''

''So they could be anyone. Were they vouched for?''

Weaver looked away.

''No,'' Clint said, ''you were so eager to get another game together that you couldn't wait, could you?''

''Look, I—''

''Never mind,'' Clint said, ''we've got to work with what we've got. Hopefully, Garr and his men will hit the bank and Quinn will kill them all. That'll clear the men in the game and you won't need me in there anymore.''

''And you can stop playing with my money.''

''Hey,'' Clint said, ''I can still just come in and watch.''

''No,'' Weaver said, ''they've got to think you're a player.''

''Have it your way, Jed,'' Clint said. ''What are we playing?''

''With seven of us in the game? Five-card stud. When somebody drops out we can mix in seven-card or draw.''

''Where's my buy-in?''

Weaver opened a desk drawer and took out an envelope that was thick with cash. He tossed it across the desk, where it landed with a thud.

''I get to keep what I win?''

''Any profit over that, you keep,'' Weaver said. ''Otherwise what you're left with comes back to me.''

''What I'm left with? If I don't win, I lose. Isn't that the game?''

''Well, if you leave the game early . . .''

''I see. Okay, if I leave early what's left comes back to you. I'm losing money while my table is closed, you know.''

''I thought you wanted to help.''

"I do," Clint said, "I do. Shall we go in and start to greet the players?"

"I'll greet them," Weaver said. "You just sit at the table as if you were the first to arrive."

"Well," Clint said, standing up and claiming his stake, "I guess I am the first to arrive."

They started for the door.

"Did you talk to Leo about not giving me away when he comes in with drinks?"

"He knows he's to act like he doesn't know you."

"What if one of these players heard I was dealing faro here?"

"If it comes up," Weaver said, "we'll just say you quit and wanted to play in this game instead."

"Okay," Clint said, "I guess we've got all the answers."

"Let's play poker," Weaver said.

THIRTY

Clint was seated at the table when the first player, Brett Ells, arrived. He was in his thirties, sandy-haired, with a pleasant, open face that Clint felt would serve him well when bluffing, if he didn't have a tell.

"A pleasure to meet you," Ells said, sitting directly across from Clint. In the center of the table were a dozen unopened packs of cards, and chips.

The players continued to arrive one by one:

Ken Block, in his fifties. He dressed badly and had an unruly shock of gray hair, but Clint had heard good things about him as a player.

Sam Wilkes, who Clint knew nothing about beyond what he saw, a man who had large hands and looked more like a farmer than a card player.

Jeff Stewart, probably the youngest player, still in his twenties. Clint wondered how he had gotten into the game at all.

And Hal Cornwall, the last to arrive. In his forties, he had neatly combed and cut hair, an equally neatly trimmed mustache, and a fussy manner. Clint was willing to bet that the man smoked very long, slender cigars. He later found out he was right.

125

"Well," Weaver said, "now that everyone has met everyone, let's get started."

They agreed on which deck of cards to open, and the players all bought chips from Weaver who, as the host, was also the bank.

They drew cards to see who would deal first, and Cornwall drew an ace and won the deal.

"My luck is good already," he said.

"Five-card stud," Weaver said. "Let's play."

Clint found out firsthand, in the first hour, just how bad Jed Weaver's luck was running—how bad it was *still* running. He'd managed to lose two huge pots with hands that normally would have won.

"Whew," Block said, "I don't recall the last time I saw anyone lose with four of a kind twice in a row."

"I don't remember the last time I saw somebody *get* four of a kind twice in a row," Ells said.

That statement hung in the air dangerously. Normally, that might sound like somebody thought somebody was cheating, but how could someone make sure they got four of a kind, and then lose with it?

"Worst luck I ever saw," Block said, shaking his head, "but it'll change."

"Yeah," Weaver said, "it'll change." But when? he thought.

They played for several hours, and Clint did well. A couple of the other players—Block and Ells—were winning more than he was, but he was doing all right. The rest were losing, but no one as heavily as Jed Weaver. And the others were losing because they weren't getting the cards. Weaver had the second best hand almost every time, a hand worth betting, but a hand that, ultimately, would lose.

When they took a break for something to eat or to drink, Clint went into Weaver's office with him.

"My God, Jed . . ." he said as they entered.

"I know," Weaver said. "It's still happening."

"I don't think I've *ever* seen this kind of a run of luck in my life," Clint said. "It's horrendous."

"So you see why I have to keep playing?"

"No, I don't," Clint said. "I don't understand why you're playing at all."

"To play it out," Weaver said. "What would you do?"

Weaver poured himself a brandy and held it up as a silent offer to Clint, who shook his head.

"If I was having a run of luck like yours," Clint said, "I wouldn't go near a deck of cards until it was over."

Weaver sat behind his desk.

"And how would you tell if it was over?"

"Play a few hands."

"A few."

"That's right."

Weaver seemed to give this some thought.

"And what would I do in the meantime?"

"Well," Clint said, "you do have a town to build, don't you?"

"You don't understand, Clint," Weaver said. "I'm a gambler."

"I think building this town was a pretty big gamble, don't you?"

"Maybe," Weaver said, "but it's not the type of gamble that sustains me. I thought it might be, you know? But it's not."

"Jed, I'm not suggesting that you quit gambling, just take a break."

"That's why you're not a professional gambler, Clint."

"Why?"

"Because you couldn't stay with it. You've got to persevere through everything, the ups, the downs—"

"Jed," Clint said, interrupting him, "have you ever had a run of luck like this before?"

"No."

"Have you ever had a run of bad luck at all before?"

"No."

"So these ups and downs you're talking about," Clint went on, "this is really the first time you've ever had downs."

"You know," Weaver said, avoiding the question, "I don't think there's a man in that room who would recommend that I stop playing."

"Of course not," Clint said. "They're playing against you. They *want* you to have bad luck."

"And you don't?"

"No."

"You're playing against me."

"With your money."

"It doesn't matter whose money you're using," Weaver said, "I think you're getting a kick out of beating me."

Clint just stared at the man.

"Jed, I never *wanted* to play in the first place."

"But you're making the most of the opportunity, aren't you?"

Clint stared at Weaver, as if seeing him for the first time. He wasn't making any sense. This losing streak was apparently affecting the way he thought.

"Jed, I'm just trying to help Quinn out, here. I happened to win a few hands—"

"Well, I don't think you should count on winning any more."

"Why not?"

"Because I'm about to start playing for keeps."

"And you haven't been up to now?"

Weaver finished his brandy and put the glass down on his desk. He stood up and shot his cuffs.

"You just watch me from here on out, my friend," Weaver said. "You're gonna see the real Jedediah Weaver."

Clint followed Weaver from the room, not at all sure he wanted to see the real Jedediah Weaver.

THIRTY-ONE

He continued to lose, only now he was bluffing, and everyone was calling his bluff.

Clint started trying to hold back, but the cards were just coming to him. He folded every time he was faced with one of Weaver's bluffs, folding a winning hand more than once. If Weaver was out of the hand already he'd go ahead and play it, and usually he won. By the time they called a halt to the game for everyone to get some rest, Clint was the big winner, and Weaver was the loser.

When they all left that back room it was morning and Leo was already making breakfast. Weaver and some of the others went to their rooms to get some sleep, but Clint wanted to eat, and so did Block and Ells. They were the only other two players who were ahead, at the moment.

Clint invited them to share a table with him, and they discussed the game.

"I only know Weaver by reputation," Block said, "but I'm surprised at the way he's been playing."

"He's pushing a run of bad luck," Clint said.

"Pushing it?" Ells asked. "He's carrying the thing on his back, if you ask me. Why doesn't he step back and take stock, take a little break?"

"He feels you have to ride out a streak of bad luck," Clint said, trying to defend his friend.

"Sometimes that's true," Block said, "but I've never seen a run like this one. I mean, losing two hands in a row with four of a kind?"

"I think," Ells said, "if it was me I'd take a year off."

"And do what?" Block asked. "I don't think I've ever taken a year off from gambling."

"There's lots of things a man could do," Ells said, "other than gambling."

"Name one," Block said.

"Traveling."

"That takes money."

"Well," Ells said, "I would assume that if a man was gambling for a living he'd put some money away to see him through a rough patch."

"How many rough patches have you been through?" Block asked.

"Several."

"And did you always have money to see you through?"

"Of course."

Block looked at Clint, who was more of his generation.

"They're a new breed today, aren't they?" he asked.

"Don't you have money put aside?" Ells asked.

"Not a dime."

"Why not?"

"I need it to live."

Both Clint and Ells studied Block for a moment. It was obvious he didn't spend the money on clothes.

"What about you, Adams?" Ells asked.

"What about me?" Clint asked. "I don't do this for a living."

"But you have money put aside, don't you?"

"Some."

"Why don't you do it for a living?" Block asked. "You seem to know your way around a deck of cards."

"Not well enough to depend on it for my future. That's for more confident men, like you fellas."

After breakfast Block announced he was going to get some sleep. Ells asked Clint if he'd have some more coffee with him, and Clint agreed.

"What's on your mind?" Clint asked.

"What makes you think something's on my mind?"

"I can read people."

"That's what makes you a good gambler."

"So let's have it."

"I think you know your way around a deck of cards better than even Mr. Block knows."

"Which means?"

"Which means you've folded several winning hands tonight—and maybe more—rather than go head-to-head with Jed Weaver."

"Is that so?"

"Oh, yes, it is," Ells said. "This is my business, Clint. I'm good at it. Something's going on here that the rest of us don't know about. Come on, spill it."

"It's nothing, really," Clint said, and then explained about the presence of Haywood Garr in town.

"So you're present just as a precaution?"

"That's right."

"That still doesn't explain why you'd fold a winning hand."

"Weaver and I are friends," Clint said. "I want to keep it that way, which is why I didn't want to play in the first place."

"I've known you to play against Luke Short, Bat Masterson, and some other men you were friends with. Do you fold winning hands against them?"

"No," Clint said, "but they are my very good friends and our rivalry at the poker table is a healthy one. Our friendship is strong enough to survive it."

"And your friendship with Weaver isn't?"

"I haven't known Jed as long or as well as I've

known, say, Bat Masterson, and I've learned things about him over the past months that I didn't know.''

''Such as?''

''Such as his inability to handle a losing streak,'' Clint said. ''This is the first one he's ever had, apparently, and he just doesn't know what to do.''

''Have you tried telling him?''

''Yes.''

''And?''

''He reminded me that he does this for a living and I don't.''

''Ah.''

They finished their coffee and both stood up.

''Well, I knew something was going on, I just didn't know what. Uh, you're not doing him any good by giving him hands, you know.''

''Maybe not.''

''And you're certainly not doing yourself any good— although you are the big winner.''

''My luck has been as good as his has been bad.''

''Yes,'' Ells said, ''I've noticed that. I'm going up against that luck, aren't I?''

''You don't seem to be doing too badly.''

''Holding my own,'' Ells said, ''waiting for the cards to come around.''

''I guess that's what Jed thinks he's doing.''

''Except that he's pushing,'' Ells said, ''and pushing hard. He *wants* it much too badly now, and that's when it never seems to come.''

Clint knew that Brett Ells was right. The more Weaver pushed against his luck, the worse it seemed to get— only could it get any worse?

THIRTY-TWO

Before turning in Clint decided to take a walk over to the bank to let Quinn know what was going on. When he walked in he didn't see Quinn or any of his guards, but he knew they were there. He waited for them to see him, and then Quinn came out of the "room" they used as a safe, since there was no real safe in the bank. A safe was not something that could easily be lugged ten thousand feet up a mountain.

"Come in here," Quinn said, opening the door to an office. "It's the president of the bank's office."

As they entered Clint said, "I thought Jed was the president of the bank."

"He is," Quinn said. "Did the game break up?"

"For a while."

"How's Jed doing?"

"Not good," Clint said. Then he added, "In fact, he's doing damn lousy, Quinn."

Clint told Quinn just how bad Weaver's luck had been, and added that he'd never seen anything like it.

"Maybe you should talk to him," Quinn suggested.

"I did."

"And?"

"He got upset," Clint said. "He thought I was challenging him."

"That's silly," Quinn said. "You didn't even want to play in the game."

"That doesn't matter," Clint said. "All that matters is that I'm in the game now."

"And how did you do?"

"I was, uh, the big winner."

"Oh, great."

"And that was with dumping a couple of hands to him when I knew he was bluffing and I had him beat."

"Jesus," Quinn said, "his luck *is* bad."

"Maybe you'd better talk to him, Quinn."

"Me? Why me?"

"He'll listen to you."

"Why?"

"He respects you."

"Not as a card player," Quinn said. "I know nothing about poker strategy, Clint. He never listens to me if it has anything to do with gambling."

"Then he's just going to keep losing."

"It's got to stop sometime."

"Theoretically," Clint said. "How's it been over here?"

"Quiet," Quinn said, "too quiet. I now agree with you, though. I think they're waiting, making us sweat. I think they're gonna come swooping down all of a sudden, but we'll be ready for them."

"I don't know what to do about the game," Clint said. "One of the players already guessed that something was wrong."

"Will he tell the others?"

"No."

"Then keep playing."

"If I do that, I don't think Jed and I will be friends much longer."

"He wouldn't end the friendship over a poker game,"
Quinn said.

"Maybe not," Clint said, heading for the door, "but
maybe I would."

Clint went back to the saloon and up to his room to turn
in. Angela hadn't been outside the saloon when he left,
so he assumed that she was staying in her own room
today, for whatever reason. He never asked her if it was
because a customer had paid for a whole night with her.
He didn't want to hear the answer.

He turned down his bed and got into it, setting his
internal clock for about three hours sleep. It usually
worked fairly well, but he was pretty tired after playing
poker all night.

He hadn't played poker in a while, and he had to admit
it felt good to have the cards coming the way they were.

In his office Jed Weaver went over his books. He was
losing heavily at poker, more heavily than he ever had
before. Several weeks ago he had realized that he was
going to have to recoup the losses somehow, and the only
way he could see to do it was to close some of the businesses he owned. His partners—the biggest being a
holder with twenty percent—wouldn't like it, but he was
in control of all the businesses, and there would be nothing they could do about it. He'd picked the two or three
smallest ones to start, so that maybe no one would notice
they were closed. Then he used the money that would
have been used to run them to finance his poker games.
Now he was checking the books again to see what other
businesses he could close, that the town could survive
without.

This run of luck was the damndest thing he'd ever run
into, but he figured all he had to do was juggle some
money here and there and wait for the streak to end.

The important thing was to stay in the game.

Of course, the people of Water Hole, the people who had all believed him when he said that the town would outlast the gold strike, probably wouldn't have liked the way he was thinking right now.

They wouldn't exactly be thrilled to find out that the founder of the town, and the man on whom the entire town depended, was putting Water Hole second to a poker game.

They wouldn't have liked that at all.

THIRTY-THREE

"I don't get it," Chuck Nyfe said.

"What don't you get?" Garr asked.

"You hustle us out of town real quick, and then you make us wait all this time to go back in."

"I explained it to you already, Chuck," Haywood Garr said. "If I have to explain it again, you're gonna make me think you're stupid or something."

Saxon and Cuddy grinned at each other across their campfire. They already knew that Chuck Nyfe was stupid. They'd been waiting for Garr to realize it, as well.

"I ain't stupid," Nyfe said, "I just don't get it."

"Explain it to him, Cuddy."

"It's simple," Cuddy said. "We wait until they think we're gone, and they feel secure, and then we go in and pick the bank."

"Or the poker game," Saxon said.

"That's another thing," Nyfe said. "Why would we rob a poker game when we could take the bank?"

"Because it's a big money poker game, Chuck," Garr said, "that's why. Sometimes you'll find more money on the table during a game like that than you will in a bank vault."

137

"And there's something else," Saxon said. "That bank ain't got a vault."

"Easy pickin's," Cuddy said.

"And only a sheriff with no deputy," Saxon said.

"What about the other man?" Nyfe asked.

Stupid, stupid, stupid kid, Garr thought. He hadn't wanted the other two to know about Clint Adams, but he couldn't tell the kid *not* to tell them, because then he would have been bursting to. He just had to hope the kid would keep his mouth shut.

Too much to hope for.

"Kid," Garr said, "go and get some more firewood."

"But we got plenty—"

"Go and get some more!"

Muttering, Chuck Nyfe left the camp.

"What other man is he talking about?" Cuddy asked.

"You didn't tell us nothing about another man," Saxon said.

"I didn't want you boys to worry."

"Is this like that time you didn't want us to worry that we was going into a town where Wyatt Earp and Doc Holliday was stayin'?" Cuddy asked.

"That was a mistake," Garr said. "I explained that to you back then."

"Uh-huh," Saxon said, "so who did you forget to tell us about this time, Haywood?"

"Well . . . there is somebody else in town we might have to deal with."

"Who?"

Garr hesitated, then said, "Clint Adams."

Both men stared at him.

"*The* Clint Adams?" Saxon asked.

"There's only one I know of."

"The Gunsmith?" Cuddy asked. "That Clint Adams?"

"That's him."

The two men looked at each other.

"This is worse than Wyatt Earp and Doc Holliday," Saxon said.

"Hey, I happen to think Holliday could have taken the Gunsmith—if he hadn't died."

"It don't matter who died, Haywood," Saxon said. "You didn't think you should tell us that Clint Adams was in town?"

"I knew you'd react this way," Garr said. "Honest, boys, the bank is easy pickings."

"Not with Clint Adams in town it ain't," Saxon said.

"But he ain't the law," Garr said. "He ain't gonna be nowheres near the bank."

"How do you know where he's gonna be?" Cuddy asked.

"I checked it out," Garr said. "Adams is in the poker game."

"The poker game that we was gonna hit if we didn't hit the bank?" Saxon asked. "That poker game?"

"That's just it," Garr said. "We're gonna hit the bank, not the game. By the time Adams knows anything happened we'll be long gone. Remember, boys, that bank ain't got no vault."

"And you're sure Adams will be in the game?" Saxon asked.

"He's there to guard it," Garr said. "That's where he'll be, all right."

"And only the sheriff will be at the bank?"

"The sheriff," Garr said, "and a couple of bank guards. Nothin' to worry about, really. Just think about it, boys. All that money and no vault, just a back room where they keep it."

"And where did you hear this?" Saxon asked.

"I heard talk on the street," Garr said, "and then I went to the bank to check it out myself."

Saxon and Cuddy exchanged a glance.

"What do you think?" Saxon asked.

"I think," Cuddy said, "a three-way split would be a lot better than a four-way split."

"Hey," Garr said, "you want to cut the kid out, that's no problem. We'll do it right after the job. How's that?"

"Well," Saxon said, "it would be a shame to leave all that money behind."

He looked at Cuddy, who said, "Yeah."

"Good," Garr said. "So you're in?"

Saxon and Cuddy exchanged another glance, and then Saxon said, "We're in."

THIRTY-FOUR

"Did you know that Jed has closed some of his businesses?"

Quinn frowned at these words from Danielle.

"Even I don't know all the businesses he owns," he admitted. "How do you know this?"

"Because a couple of his so-called 'partners' don't have wives, so they stopped in here to cry on somebody's shoulder."

"Which ones did he close?" Quinn asked.

She named a couple, one of which was the hardware store.

"I saw that the place closed a couple of weeks ago," Quinn said, "but I didn't think . . . He started that long ago?"

"Several weeks. Do you know why he's doing this?"

Quinn shrugged.

"I could only guess, but maybe they weren't doing as well as—"

"That's very loyal of you, Ollie," she said, cutting him off.

They were in her room, away from the prying ears and eyes of the other girls. They had not gone to bed. She had attacked him—if attacked was the proper word—

with this news as soon as they were alone.

"What is?"

"Making excuses for your friend."

"I wasn't making excuses," Quinn said. "You asked me if I knew why he'd closed them. I was just guessing."

"Well, try this as a guess," she said. "He's losing a lot of money gambling, and it's starting to cost the town."

Quinn remained silent.

"He is losing a lot of money lately, isn't he?"

"Well, yes—"

"And he's got to replace it from somewhere."

"So you think he's closing businesses and using the money from them to . . . to keep playing poker."

"Exactly," she said. She walked to the window and looked out. "That has already cost some people their homes, Ollie. How many more before the whole town starts to suffer?"

"I think maybe you're jumping to conclusions, Martha—"

"I don't think so." She turned to face him, putting her back to the window now. "And I'll tell you why. I haven't seen any money from him in weeks."

"What?"

"That's right," she said. "He keeps telling me that operating expenses are getting high for some of the businesses. He'll get me my cut when he can. He was telling some of the others that, too, and then he pulled their businesses out from under them." She walked to him, stopping just a few feet away. "Is that gonna happen to me, Ollie? If it is, I'd like to know about it."

"Martha," Quinn said, "this was one of the first places Jed put together. I don't think he's gonna pull it out from under you."

"You don't think?" She grabbed both of his arms. "Could you find out for me, Ollie? I need to know if me and the girls are gonna end up without jobs, and without a place to stay.''

''Jed wouldn't do that—''

''He did it to Mr. and Mrs. Evans,'' she said. ''He closed their shop right out from under them.''

''I was wondering why they left . . .''

''Without warning, Ollie,'' she went on, ''he did it without warning.''

He took her into his arms.

''You told me you'd take care of us, Ollie,'' she said into his chest.

''I know I did, Martha, and I meant it. I'll talk to Jed.''

''You will?'' she asked, pulling her head back and looking up at him. ''You will?''

''Sure, I will.''

''When?''

''Soon.''

''Today?''

''Today . . . or tomorrow,'' he said, pulling her to him again. ''Soon.''

They stood that way for a while and then he asked, ''How did you know about the Evanses?''

''Mr. Evans came here to cry on someone's shoulder, too,'' she said.

THIRTY-FIVE

"Why are you pressuring me, Ollie!" Weaver shouted from behind his desk. It was the next morning and Quinn had finally broached the subject of Weaver closing down businesses.

"I'm not pressuring you, Jed," Quinn said. "I was just asking—"

"Do you want to tell me how to run my business now?" Weaver asked.

"You know I'd never do that, Jed—"

"Are you afraid I'm gonna take that badge back? Is that it?"

"The badge doesn't mean anything to me, Jed."

"Then what is it, Quinn?" Weaver asked. "Why are you questioning my decisions now?"

"I'm not . . . really, Jed," Quinn said, "I was just wondering . . . why you closed down some of the businesses . . ."

"I don't know who you've been talking to, Ollie," Weaver said, "but I'll tell you, some of the businesses were not doing well, and they were putting a strain on the others, okay? If you're worried about the Palace going under, don't. We're doing fine."

"Are there any, uh, other businesses that you might be closing down?"

"Like what, Ollie?" Weaver asked from behind his desk. He had a deck of cards spread out on the top of the desk, as if he were trying to figure them out. "Do you have a special one in mind?"

"I was just wondering about the social club," Quinn said. "Are you gonna close it down?"

"The social club," Weaver said, looking down at his desk as if he had the answer there. "The social club . . . well, I don't know, Ollie. Do you think I should close it down?"

Quinn shrugged and said, "It's your business, Jed."

"That's right, Ollie," Weaver said, "it's mine, and if it suits me to close it down, I will. Is there some special reason you're interested in the social club?"

"You know there is."

"Oh, yeah, that's right, you and Martha—I mean, Danielle—have something going, don't you? Well, hey, if I closed it down she'd have more time for you, wouldn't she?"

"Why are you doing this, Jed?" Quinn asked. "Is this long losing streak turning you mean? Is that it?"

"This 'losing streak,' as you call it, is about to end, my friend," Weaver said, "you just wait and see."

"You're kiddin' yourself, Jed," Quinn said.

"What? What did you say?"

"You'd better think long and hard about what you're doing," Quinn said, heading for the door. "You're playing with people's lives."

"Do you mean the people who live in this town?" Weaver called after him. "Hey, they live in my town, their *lives* are mine to play with!"

Quinn didn't hear the last of it because he was gone. Weaver slammed his fist down on the desk in anger. He *would* close the social club down except for one thing— next to the Palace, it was making the most money.

"Everybody's tryin' to tell me what to do," he muttered. He picked up some of the cards and looked at them critically. He held up an ace of spades and said to it, "You've got to turn. You've got to!"

THIRTY-SIX

Later in the day, during a break in the game, Leo brought Clint a message.

"Mr. Quinn says he's got to talk to you."

"I'm in the middle of the game, Leo."

"He says it's urgent, when you get a chance."

"Is he at the bank?"

"Yes."

"Tell him I'll try and get over there."

"How's the game going?"

"Everyone seems to be having a normal ebb and flow of luck except for Jed," Clint said. "His luck is still sour."

"Did you hear what I heard?"

"About what?"

"That the boss is closing down some of his businesses and using the money so he can keep playing?"

"No, I hadn't heard that," Clint said. "Is that what Quinn wants to talk about?"

"Maybe."

"Well, even if it's true," Clint said, "they're his businesses, he can do what he wants to with them."

"But it could affect the whole town."

"Maybe," Clint said, "but that's his, too, isn't it?"

"I guess."

"Leo, have you noticed how slow it is around here lately?"

"I sure have."

"What have you heard about the mines?"

Leo rubbed his jaw and hesitated.

"You have heard something, haven't you?"

"Some of the men have been grumbling, saying they're not taking as much out of the mines as they had been," Leo said.

"This was supposed to be a huge strike," Clint said. "What's going on?"

Leo shrugged and said, "I don't know. Maybe Mr. Quinn wants to talk about that, too."

Clint looked at the time. He had a half hour before the game restarted.

"I'll take a walk over to the bank now," Clint said. "If I'm not back when the game starts tell the players I won't be long."

"Okay."

Clint put down his beer, left the saloon, and headed for the bank.

Earlier that morning Haywood Garr kicked awake his three partners and said, "It's time."

Ollie Quinn couldn't stop thinking about Weaver's reactions to his questions that morning. He'd always known Jed Weaver to be fair and open. The reaction that morning was by someone else, not the Jed Weaver he knew. He had to find out from Clint Adams if he thought Weaver was acting erratically. As a gambler who had never had a losing streak before, maybe Weaver was being pushed over the edge. Maybe the pressure was becoming too much for him.

Quinn looked over at the two men he had with him, guarding the bank. They were all in the "vault" room and

it was hot in there. He and both men were sweating. He'd
sent one man back to the saloon, today, but there really
was no need for that, either. Each night there seemed to be
less and less reason to have guards in the Palace, because
there were less and less men there. He hadn't yet heard of
anyone pulling up stakes and leaving his claim, but clearly
something was going wrong.

"Mr. Quinn," one of the guards said, "I got to go out
and get some air."

"I was just gonna say the same thing," the other guard
said.

"Go ahead, then," Quinn said. "Go out the back,
though, so nobody sees you."

"Should we go together?" the first guard said.

"Why not?" Quinn said. "What's gonna happen if
you're gone ten minutes?"

Both men shrugged and left the room, taking their ri-
fles with them.

Quinn looked around at the bags of gold and boxes of
cash that were on the shelves that lined the walls. He was
shocked to see how much less there was these days.
There was a time when this room had been full, and now
it was only half so. What more did he need? What other
signs? Apparently, Water Hole was in decline, and Jed
Weaver closing down businesses left and right was not
helping any. The Gambler had finally taken over from
the Town Builder. This was something Ollie Quinn had
feared from the beginning. He hadn't thought that a gambler was a good choice to be a town builder because,
sooner or later, it would come down to a choice of one
or the other.

And the gambler would always choose gambling.

Haywood Garr rode into town with his three partners,
Saxon, Cuddy, and Nyfe, and stopped just at the end of
town.

"Okay," he said, drawing his gun. "We go in hard

and fast. We hit them before they know what's happening."

"And if that sheriff shows up?" Nyfe asked.

"Put a hole in him!" Garr said.

"Kill him?"

"That's right," he said, "kill him. Now let's go!"

THIRTY-SEVEN

They struck quickly, riding up to the bank and leaping from their horses. Garr, Saxon, and Cuddy tossed the reins of their mounts to Nyfe, whose job it was to make sure the horses were there when the bank robbers came out.

However, Clint happened to be walking toward the bank at that moment, instead of being back at the saloon, getting ready for the game to restart.

The timing couldn't have been worse for Haywood Garr and company.

As far as Haywood Garr was concerned, as he, Saxon, and Cuddy went into the bank, the timing couldn't have been better. As far as he was concerned, Clint Adams was at that moment tossing money into a pot at a poker table, and the sheriff was off doing his job somewhere. With only some bank guards to face, this robbery should be easy to pull off.

As they entered the bank with guns drawn, Garr shouted, "Everybody down on the ground." To make his point he fired one shot into the air.

• • •

153

Out back the two guards were cooling off when they heard the shot. One of them reached for the back door to open it, and they realized that the door had locked behind them.

"Damn it!" one of them swore, and they started running around the building.

Ollie Quinn heard the shot and came barreling out of the vault room. He saw the tellers on the floor behind their cages, and one man—Cuddy—was coming around to join them. Quinn wasted no time and shot Cuddy in the chest with his Colt.

Outside Clint approached the front of the bank, and Chuck Nyfe saw him coming. The young man went for his gun, but never had a chance to draw it. Clint produced his gun first, fired, and killed the man with one shot. As he fell to the ground Nyfe released his hold on the three horses, and they ran off, spooked by the shot.

The two guards came around from the side of the building at that moment and Clint shouted to them, "Stay out here!"

He ran into the bank.

Quinn came around from behind the tellers' cages and found himself facing two men, Garr and Saxon.

Garr was satisfied to see Quinn but no guards.

"Big mistake, lawman!" he said.

But as he and Saxon prepared to fire, Clint Adams rushed through the front door and shouted, "Garr!"

Garr turned and drew while Saxon turned his gun on Quinn. The air was filled with the sound of four shots. Two men fell to the ground and one staggered back, wounded.

Clint and Quinn watched as the bodies of the four bank robbers were carried away to the undertaker's.

''How's your shoulder?'' Clint asked Quinn.

''It's not bad,'' Quinn said. ''I'd be a lot worse off if you hadn't come along. What brought you over here?''

''Leo said you wanted to talk to me.''

''I did,'' Quinn said. ''Your timing was perfect. Thanks.''

''Don't mention it.''

The two guards were back on duty inside the vault room, with instructions to stay there no matter how hot they got.

''Come on,'' Clint said, ''I'll walk over to the doc with you and you can tell me what's on your mind.''

''Walk me to Martha's,'' Quinn said. ''She can take care of this as well as our so-called doctor—or do you want to get back to the game?''

''Now that Garr and his men have been taken care of, there's no need for me to go back to the game,'' Clint said.

''Won't they be upset that you're leaving while you're ahead?''

''I'll toss the money back into the pot,'' Clint said. ''They won't mind so much then.''

''I guess not. You know,'' Quinn said, ''my guards were out back—locked out, as it happened—and if you hadn't come along—''

''But I did,'' Clint said. ''The timing worked out. Now we can forget about it and move on.''

''To other problems,'' Quinn said.

''Like?''

''Like I think Jed's gone over the edge, Clint,'' Quinn said. ''You heard what he's been doing?''

''From Leo.''

''I've been friends with Jed a long time, but this ain't right.''

''Quinn,'' Clint said, ''what about the strike? Is it petering out?''

"Something's gone wrong," Quinn said, "and I don't know if Water Hole is going to survive."

Clint hoped it would. He'd been looking forward to being in on the birth of a town, not the birth *and* death of a town within the same year.

THIRTY-EIGHT

Danielle cleaned the wound in her room, with the help of Angela, while Clint stood by, watching.

"What have you been hearing from the miners, Danielle?" Clint asked.

"Angela?" Danielle said while she concentrated on Quinn's bandage. The bullet had furrowed through his skin and kept on going; there was no hole, and no damage to anything vital.

"Some of them have been saying they're gonna pull up stakes and try California," Angela said.

"Their claims are drying up?" Clint asked.

"In a hurry," she said.

"Why didn't you tell me you were hearing this?" Clint asked.

"Or me?" Danielle asked.

"We talked it over," Angela said, "me and the other girls, and we didn't want to start a panic."

"It sounds to me like Jed Weaver has already panicked," Danielle said.

"Maybe," Clint said, "but maybe about something else."

"His losing streak?" Danielle asked.

"But it's starting to affect the town now," Quinn said.

"Can this town survive the strike drying up," Angela asked, "and Jed's losing streak?"

"I guess that's the big question, isn't it?" Clint said.

Danielle sat back, finished with the wound. She dropped the bloody rags into the basin of water Angela was holding and turned to face Clint.

"Well, my answer is no," she said. "I'm for pulling up stakes, myself."

"What about us?" Angela asked.

"If I leave," Danielle said, "as many as you girls want can come with me. Or you can stay, Angela, and take over for me."

"I don't want to run a house," Angela said. "That's too much responsibility for me."

"You're smart enough to do it," Clint said.

"I'm smart enough to know I don't want to do it," she said. "No, if you leave, Dany, I'm going with you, and so will the other girls."

Danielle looked at Quinn.

"This," he said to her, "is something we have to talk about alone."

Clint looked at Angela and said, "That's our cue to leave. Quinn, I'll talk to you later."

"Thanks again for your help . . . Clint."

"Sure."

He and Angela went out and closed the door behind them.

"Do you think he'll leave with her?" Angela asked.

"I don't know," Clint said. "He's pretty loyal to Jed, but this isn't the Jed he's known for many years."

"I think he loves Dany," Angela said. "I think he'll go with her. It's so romantic."

"Uh-huh."

She slapped his arm and said, "Don't be a fool, I don't expect the same thing from you, any more than you'd expect it from me."

"No?" Clint asked, trying not to show his relief.

"No—and you don't have to sound so relieved."

"I thought I was hiding it well."

"I have to get rid of this," she said, indicating the basin of bloody water in her hand. "Can you stay around?"

"I'm afraid not," he said. "I'm going to have to talk to Jed."

"About all this?"

"About some of it, anyway," Clint said. "Listen, don't tell the girls—"

"They have a right to know what's going on, Clint," she said, cutting him off. "I'm sorry, but I'm going to tell them."

"Well, all right," he said, "but try to keep it in the house, all right?"

"I'll do my best."

He kissed her shortly and said, "Come by later?"

"Sure," she said. "Who knows? It could be the last time."

Clint returned to the Crystal Palace. It wasn't crowded, but what patrons were there were buzzing about the attempted bank robbery.

"We heard what happened," Leo said to Clint. "Did you get them all?"

"We got them."

"Dead?"

Clint nodded.

"You okay?"

"I'm fine."

"And Mr. Quinn?"

"He lost some skin on his left shoulder, but he's okay. Did anyone from the game come out to see what was going on?" Clint asked.

"No, but I don't think they could hear the shots from back there."

"Oh, I think they heard them," Clint said, "they just

didn't think they were important enough to stop the game."

"What are you gonna do?"

"I'm going to stop the game," Clint said.

THIRTY-NINE

When Clint walked in on the game, Weaver looked up and said, "It's about time. You have all the money on the table."

Clint walked to his place, where his chips were stacked, and pushed it all into the pot of a game that was already going on.

"What are you doing?" Weaver asked.

"I'm out of the game," he said. "The rest of you can play for my money."

"The shooting?" Weaver asked.

"The bank."

"And?"

"We stopped the robbery."

"Then you can sit down and play."

"No, that means I can stop playing, remember?" Clint asked.

"What's going on?" Block asked.

"I think what Clint is trying to say," Brett Ells opined, "is that he's out of the game."

"Right on the money, Brett," Clint said. He looked at Weaver. "Finish this hand and then take a break. We have to talk."

"We just came off a break," one of the other players complained.

"You'll have to take another one," Clint said, "or play around Weaver for a while." To Weaver he said, "That might actually help your luck."

"Finish the hand," Weaver said, scowling.

They were playing seven-card stud and had one card to go. Clint noticed that Weaver had a pair of aces on the table, while Ells had two pair. The dealer was Block and he doled out the last card.

"A hundred," Ells said.

Two players folded and Weaver said, "A hundred, and two hundred better."

The pot was significantly bigger than it had been when Clint entered the room.

Another player dropped and then Block said, "Call."

The play moved to Ells who said, "The way your luck has been going, Jed, I've got to hit you once. Three hundred better."

"Five hundred better than that," Weaver said, and as he pushed the chips into the center of the table Clint wondered which closed-down businesses they represented.

"I'm out," Block said.

Ells pursed his lips, thought a moment, then shrugged and said, "Call."

"Aces full," Weaver said, flipping over his hole cards to reveal another ace and two sevens.

"That beats my full house," Ells said, and turned his cards over.

"Come to Poppa," Weaver said, raking in the chips, including Clint's. He didn't seem to care at that moment that a lot of it was his own money. "Clint, you sly dog, you might actually have changed my luck by dropping out of the game."

"Let's go to your office," Clint said, "and talk about your luck."

• • •

Weaver was in good spirits as they entered his office.

"What's on your mind?"

"I quit."

"What? Why?"

"Because you've got a dying town on your hands, Jed, and I don't want to be around to see it."

"What are you talking about, a dying town?"

"You know what I'm talking about. You've been closing down businesses to keep playing cards. Well, I think you should just shut down the town all at once instead of killing it piece by piece."

"All I've been doing is juggling money—"

"And playing with people's lives."

"Now you sound like Quinn."

"Quinn got shot trying to protect the bank—your bank."

"Is he all right?"

"He'll be fine, but somehow I don't think he'll be around much longer."

Weaver frowned.

"Quinn wouldn't quit on me."

"If I'm any judge of people," Clint said, "he already has."

"It's that bitch, isn't it?"

"No," Clint said, "I think it's you. You've changed, Jed, and a lot of people don't like it."

"What do I care what people like?" Weaver asked. "The Crystal Palace is doing fine, and I can find another woman to run the social club if you're telling me what I think you're telling me."

"I'm telling you that Danielle is ready to leave, and when she does all of the girls are going with her," Clint said, "and so is Quinn."

"I'll believe that when I hear it from him."

As if on cue there was a knock at the door.

"Maybe," Clint said, "you're about to hear it right now."

FORTY

Weaver shouted for whoever it was to come in. The door opened, and both Quinn and Danielle entered.

"Well, well, both of you," Weaver said. "This is a pleasure."

"I'm leaving, Jed," Quinn said without preamble.

"You're gonna let this woman come between us, huh, Ollie? This whore?"

Quinn fought to keep his temper in check. "Jed, you've changed. You're not the man I followed here, the man I've been able to be loyal to for as long as I've known you."

Weaver came around his desk and stood nose to nose with the bigger man.

"You call taking off with the first cheap floozie that comes along being lo—" He didn't get a chance to finish. Quinn backhanded him across the mouth. Weaver staggered back, and only bumping into his desk kept him from falling down. His lips were dripping blood down his chin. He righted himself, wiped his face with the back of his hand, and stared at the bright crimson stain left there.

"Thanks, Jed," Quinn said.

"For what?" Weaver asked.

165

"For making it easy for me to leave," Quinn said. "Martha, the girls, and I are all going. You won't have to close down the social club, we'll do it for you."

"You owe me money, Jed," Martha/Danielle said.

He stared at her and said, "I don't have it."

"I didn't think you did—unless it's on that poker table in there."

Weaver only glared at her.

"Don't worry," she said, "I don't want your poker stake. Luckily, I've been putting money away since I got here."

"You've been stealing from me?"

"I've been putting *my* money away."

"And so have I," Quinn said. "We've got enough to get us to San Francisco." He looked at Clint. "That's where we're going."

"Good luck to you," Clint said.

He and Quinn shook hands, and then Clint kissed Danielle.

"When are you leaving?" Clint asked.

"In the morning," Danielle said. "Angela said to tell you she'll see you later, to say good-bye."

"I'll be waiting," Clint said.

Quinn and Danielle both looked at Weaver, who was still leaning on his desk, but there was nothing left to say to him.

They left.

"Bastard," Weaver said, wiping his mouth again. "Bitch."

"Two of your best friends, once," Clint said.

"Not my friends."

"You really had something going here for a while, Jed," Clint said, shaking his head, "but you let a losing streak bring it all crumbling down around you."

"Nothing's crumbling," Weaver said, "and the losing streak is over. You saw me take that big hand in there. It's over."

"That remains to be seen," Clint said. "I actually wish you luck. You're going to need it."

"I don't need your luck," Weaver said. "I don't need Quinn, or Danielle, or anybody. I've got the Palace, and I've got my own luck."

He straightened up finally, pulled a handkerchief from his pocket, and blotted his lips. He held the cloth there while he poured himself a glass of brandy. By the time he finished the brandy the bleeding had stopped.

He turned and looked at Clint.

"I've got a game to play."

"I'll be out of my room by morning, Jed."

"That's fine," Weaver said. "I'm not kicking you out, you're leaving on your own."

"Yes, I am."

Weaver walked past Clint and left the office. Clint walked to the door and watched the man cross the room and enter the room where his poker game was waiting. He hoped that Weaver's luck had indeed changed from bad to good.

He was going to need all the good luck he could get.

FORTY-ONE

Clint and Angela spent their last night in Water Hole together. When she first appeared in front of the saloon he took her upstairs and made love to her right away. After that they lay together a long while and talked.

"Where will you go?" she asked.

"I'll probably head down to Texas to see my friend Rick Hartman, in a town called Labyrinth. I've been here longer than I've been anywhere, for a while. After that I'll just travel around."

"Will you get to San Francisco?"

"I'm sure I will."

"Will you come and see me?"

"If you let me know where you are," he said, "definitely."

She snuggled closer to him, and he could feel her breath on his skin. He slid one hand down her back to her buttocks, which were smooth and firm.

"What do you think of all this, Clint?" she asked suddenly. "What went wrong?"

"A gambler tried to do something other than gamble," he said, "and he couldn't."

"Do you mean that Jed should have given up gambling altogether?"

"If he really wanted to build a town, yes," he said. "This kind of endeavor takes all a man's time and effort. He just wasn't willing to give it."

"And the gold?"

"All gold strikes dry up eventually," he said. "This one is doing it a lot earlier than people thought—too early for the town to survive."

"Maybe he'll be able to keep it together."

"He'll keep this place open for a while," Clint said, "but I'm sure the rest of it will dry up around him and fade away."

"So what will he do when there's nobody here?" she wondered aloud.

"I don't know," Clint said. "Maybe the miners will be around a little longer, and others will come to try their hand at the dried-up claims, just in case there's a little more. Jed will keep afloat for a while, but for it to happen he'll need one other thing."

"What's that?"

"He'll need for his luck to change," Clint said, "drastically."

"And will it?"

"It will change," Clint said. "Just like all mines dry up, luck never stays good or bad. The question is, *when* will it change?"

"When do you think?"

He shook his head.

"I can't tell, Angela," he said. "Luck's a funny thing. It could be today, tomorrow, next week, next month, or even next year."

"I've never been part of something like this before," she said. "It's sad to see it die."

"Yes, it is."

"But I'm glad I got a chance to meet you."

"That reminds me," he said, sliding one finger along the crease between her butt cheeks.

"Of what?"

"We haven't finished saying good-bye."

"We haven't?"

"Not by a long shot," he said.

They moved together, legs entwining, kissing and moving their hands over each other. He pushed her onto her back and began to kiss her breasts, nibble her nipples.

Breasts, he decided, were his favorite part of a woman's body, and he'd never met a woman who became impatient with the amount of attention he paid them. He lingered over Angela's firm mounds for a long time, bringing moans and cries from her, before gradually moving down her body. Finally, his mouth was pressed to her wetness, and his tongue and lips played avidly on her until she tensed and cried out, arching her back and drumming her heels on the mattress.

"Oooh!" she moaned after a few moments. "Come up here, quick. I want you inside of me."

He slid up her body until he was nose to nose with her. She reached between them for his rigid penis and guided it into her.

"Slow," she said, "put it in slow, and move slow. I want this to last and last."

"It's a long night, Angela," he said, reaching beneath her to cup her fine buttocks in his hands, "and we can use it all to say good-bye properly."

"Then let's use it. . . ."

In the morning he woke her with butterfly kisses on her eyes and cheeks, and then moved lower and lower until she was drumming her heels on the bed again. After that she pushed him onto his back and returned the favor, kissing him and stroking him until he was ready to burst, and then finally mounting him, taking him inside so he could explode there.

FORTY-TWO

They stood outside the Crystal Palace in the morning as the buckboard pulled to a stop in front. Quinn was driving it, with Danielle—who was back to being called Martha—on the seat with him. The other girls were in the back.

"Time to go, Angela," Martha said.

Angela turned and kissed Clint long and hard while the others girls whooped and hollered. Then suddenly one of them said, "I want some of that," and they were all off the buckboard and taking turns kissing Clint soundly. Finally, as they all piled back in, Clint stepped closer and kissed Martha.

"Good luck," he said, shaking hands with Quinn. "Take care of each other."

"We will," Quinn said. "When are you leaving?"

"In a few minutes."

"If you see Jed," Quinn said, "tell him . . ."

"Tell him what?"

Quinn shook his head.

"Never mind," he said. "I don't have anything to say to him."

Clint watched the buckboard drive away, all of the

girls waving good-bye. He watched it until it was out of sight, then went inside for one last breakfast of Leo's.

Clint sat back and rubbed his stomach as Leo poured some more coffee.

"Leo, you outdid yourself today."

"Well," the big bartender said, "I figure this one's gotta hold you for a while. It'll probably be a long time before you get a breakfast like one of mine again."

"If I could find a woman who could cook like you," Clint said, "I'd probably marry her—well, maybe I wouldn't go that far."

Clint stood up and put out this hand.

"Take care of yourself," he said, as they shook hands.

"You, uh, don't want to talk to the boss again before you go?"

"No," Clint said, "I said what I had to say. Did his luck change last night?"

"No," Leo said. "After he took the pot with your money in it, he didn't take another one all night."

"It'll change," Clint said. "Eventually, it'll change."

"I hope so."

"What are you going to do, Leo?"

"Me? I guess I'll stay here until there's no more here to stay at."

"Good luck."

Clint left the Crystal Palace and walked to the livery to saddle Duke. When he got there another man was saddling his horse, as well. There was a bedroll on the back of his saddle.

"Packin' it in, huh?" the man asked.

"Time to move on," Clint said.

"Yeah, me, too," the man said. "This strike has about petered out."

"Are you sure?"

"Sure enough to give up my claim," the man said. He patted his saddlebags. "I'm gettin' out with some dust left for a stake. This place is gonna be dead in a matter of weeks.''

Clint nodded and said, ''That's what I'm afraid of.''

He mounted Duke and rode out, taking the opposite direction of the departing miner. This was just the beginning of the exodus, he knew. Before long most of the buildings would be vacant, the claims would be abandoned, and Water Hole would be a ghost town.

He wished Jed Weaver luck.

EPILOGUE

Six months later, Denver

Clint hadn't expected to be back in Denver just six months after he'd left Water Hole, Colorado, but there he was, staying at the Denver House again. He'd been called to Denver to help his friend, Talbot Roper. The private detective had needed a man he could trust to watch his back, and he didn't think he could make a better choice than Clint Adams. Clint, always ready to help a friend, especially a good friend like Roper, had agreed. There were three men Clint Adams would do just about anything for: Bat Masterson, Wyatt Earp, and Talbot Roper, and he knew they felt the same. When he was alive, Wild Bill Hickok was also on that list.

So Clint had come to Denver and had helped Roper out of a jam, and now, with that over and done with, he was ready to leave Denver behind again.

Coincidence was something Clint Adams did not like, but he knew there was little you could do about it when it poked its head into your life—like now. He saw a familiar figure walking across the lobby floor of the Denver House, heading for the front desk—apparently preparing to check in. Over a year earlier the man had approached him while he was at the front desk, so now he returned the favor.

"Checking in or out?" he asked, coming up behind Jed Weaver.

Weaver turned and gave Clint a surprised look.

"How are you, Jed?"

"Surprised."

"You can't be so surprised to see me in Denver," Clint said.

"I'm surprised you'd even talk to me after the way I treated you."

"The way I figure it," Clint said, "you were under a lot of strain."

"You can say that again."

"So? In or out?"

"In. What about you?"

"I've been here a few days. I was trying to decide whether or not to stay an extra day."

"Don't let me influence you."

"Well," Clint said, "if you would have dinner with me tonight and tell me what happened after I left you in Water Hole, I'd consider staying one extra night."

"Done," Weaver said. "Talking about it will probably do me a lot of good. Let me get checked in and I'll meet you here in the lobby in, oh, two hours?"

"That's fine."

"We can eat here."

"That suits me, too."

"See you then."

As Weaver walked away, carrying his own bag up the stairs to the second floor, even Clint was surprised he had spoken to the man—but it had never occurred to him not to. Sure, Weaver had done everything to push not only him away in Water Hole, but Ollie Quinn as well. The simple fact of the matter was, Clint had thought about Weaver often since then, wondering what had hap-

pened after they all left town, and here was his chance
to find out.

What was one more night?

Clint was waiting in the lobby when Jed Weaver came
down, looking resplendent in a dark suit and white shirt,
his hair neatly combed and his cheeks freshly scraped.
They went into the dining room and were seated immediately. Both were well known at the hotel.

"So what brings you to Denver?" Clint asked.

"What else? A game."

"Ah."

"Don't suppose you'd be interested in playing?"

"No," Clint said, and he was thankful that Weaver
did not pursue it any further. He would never again play
in a game with Jed Weaver. He had at least learned that
from the debacle in Water Hole.

The waiter came over and took their order, then left
them alone to talk while they waited for their food.

"What brings you here?"

"A friend asked me to come to town and help him."

"And did you . . . help him, I mean?"

"Oh, yes," Clint said, "everything went well and he
accomplished what he set out to do."

"Unlike me, huh?"

"I didn't say it."

"No," Weaver said, "I did. Believe me, Clint, I look
back at that whole affair with embarrassment. What made
me think I could build a town? I'm a gambler, pure and
simple."

"Is that what you learned?"

"That's one thing," Weaver said. "The other thing I
learned is how to better deal with a losing streak. You
tried to tell me, and so did Ollie Quinn, but I wouldn't
listen. I had to learn for myself."

"Have you heard from Ollie?"

"No," Weaver said. "I went to San Francisco once,

but apparently he's not as forgiving as you are. He wouldn't talk to me—not that I blame him."

"All right, Jed," Clint said, suddenly impatient, "give. What happened after I left Water Hole?"

"After you left, and Ollie and Martha left, it died, just like you thought it would."

"It didn't just die," Clint said.

"No," Weaver said. "After you left I embarrassed myself some more in that poker game. It lasted another two days, and when it was over I was a beaten man. The other players all left and I poked my head out and saw a dying town. People were leaving in droves. The mines had dried up. I had looted my own town to support my game. I tried to keep the Palace going after that. A few stubborn miners hung on, but finally they all left and I was left with a ghost town and an empty Crystal Palace."

"And Leo."

"Leo was great," Weaver said, shaking his head. "He stayed with me until the end."

"What happened to him?"

"That's right, you wouldn't know that," Weaver said. "Well, he got it into his head that he could still fight."

"He once told me he never lost a fight. Was that true?"

"It was—until a couple of months ago."

"He finally lost one, huh?"

"One was all it took," Weaver said. "It happened in Alaska."

"What happened?"

"He was beaten to death by a man twenty years younger than him."

"Leo's dead?" Clint felt a coldness in the pit of his stomach.

"I'm afraid so."

"Damn it!" Clint said. He had liked the old boxer—obviously, from the way he was feeling, even more than he'd thought.

"Hey, I'm sorry," Weaver said. "I didn't realize you liked him that much."

"Leo and his breakfasts, and his loyalty to you, those are some of the good memories I took away from Water Hole."

"I have some good memories, too," Weaver said, "but they were early on. You know, once I fell into that losing streak I couldn't think straight. Nothing went right; I made all the wrong decisions. I lost my town, my Palace, and my friends."

"A losing streak is a hard thing to deal with sometimes," Clint said.

"I always thought I was lucky, you know? Lucky never to have had a losing streak. The truth is, that was the worst thing that could have happened to me. Everybody has to learn how to lose, and I never did."

"Well, it sounds like you learned from it," Clint said. "That's the important thing."

"I learned," Weaver said, "but I paid too high a price."

At that point the waiter appeared with their dinners, and since they were both hungry—sometimes talking did that to you—they both turned their attention to their steaks.

After dinner they went into the bar. They got a beer each and grabbed a table in the back, where they could continue to talk.

"When's your game start?" Clint asked.

"About an hour and a half. I have time for one beer."

"How's it going these days?"

"You mean the poker? I'm winning again—for the most part. You know, you'd think after all that happened I'd give it up, but I realized something—I can't. It's in my blood. I just have to realize that this is all I want to do. It was madness for a gambler to try and build a town.

Quinn tried to tell me that right in the beginning, and I wouldn't listen.''

''Do you think he'll ever speak to you again?''

''I hope so.''

''How's he doing?''

''Great. He and Martha own a hotel in San Francisco. Angela works for them. Both she and Martha gave up working in whorehouses.''

''And the other girls?''

''I don't know what happened to them. I think Angela's the only one who's with them.''

''I'm glad they're still together.''

''So am I. They were good for each other. Boy, some of the things I said . . .'' Weaver shook his head.

''Maybe, in time, he'll forget.''

''He won't forget,'' Weaver said. ''Quinn doesn't forget, but maybe he'll forgive me, and we'll be able to be friends again. I know one thing.''

''What?''

''I don't ever again want to command the kind of loyalty I got from Quinn and from Leo. I don't deserve it, and I don't know what to do with it.''

Clint was surprised. The last thing he'd expected from Jed Weaver was humility.

''Yeah, I know,'' Weaver said, as if reading Clint's mind, ''it surprises me, too.''

''What?''

''That I could be humble—well, I'm not *humble*, but I *was* humbled by the whole experience. I'll never again try to be something I'm not cut out to be.''

They finished their beers and walked out of the bar together. They stopped in front of the hotel before parting company, Weaver to his game, and Clint to his room.

''Tell me something,'' Clint said as they shook hands.

''What?''

''You said you came out of that game a beaten man, and that everything died around you, but here you are, gambling again. How did you come up with a stake after that?''

"I had a little money left,'' Weaver said, "so I hired some miners who were leaving town to knock down the Crystal Palace.''

"That must have been hard to watch.''

"It was,'' Weaver said, "but as soon as it was knocked down my luck changed.''

"How so?''

"You know those miners were always coming into my place with their gold dust, right?''

"Right.''

"Well, a lot of it fell through the floorboards, little by little, and it built up.''

"You mean . . .''

Weaver nodded.

"I pulled up those boards and took two thousand dollars in gold dust out of that place. That was my stake.''

"Well,'' Clint said, shaking his head, "that's what I call a change of luck.''

Watch for

VIGILANTE JUSTICE

202nd novel in the exciting GUNSMITH series
from Jove

Coming in November!